REAWAKENING

A Novel by

ERVIN GRANT

A division of Squire Publishers, Inc.
4500 College Blvd.
Leawood, KS 66211
1/888/888-7696

Copyright 2001
Printed in the United States

ISBN: 1-58597-072-7

Library of Congress Control No. 2001-131262

A division of Squire Publishers, Inc.
4500 College Blvd.
Leawood, KS 66211
1/888/888-7696

ACKNOWLEDGMENT

I wish to express appreciation to many of my friends and acquaintances who have, perhaps unwittingly, awakened me to an awareness of a spiritual dimension to an otherwise traditional religion. A succession of ministers of the El Dorado, Kansas, First United Methodist Church have instilled in me a background of searching for meaning and have encouraged the quest for a new level of consciousness in matters of faith. This quest has been aided by the ideas of those insightful "pilgrims" who regularly gathered at our house to discuss new dimensions of spirituality. But most of all, I owe so much to the ideas and personal experience of my wife, Mary Jo, who has so ably exemplified a vital, growing Christian faith, and who has overcome so many physical and emotional obstacles to become a spiritual advisor to so many. I also wish to acknowledge he skillful editing of Cynthia Snider who has contributed to the quality of this work, and the faithful reproduction of the final manuscript by Arlys Gilchrist.

The motivation for writing this book came from a dream or vision I experienced while my wife and I were attending a seminar at Pecos, New Mexico, at which the presenters were Morton Kelsey and John Sanford. This vision told me I was to compose and disseminate some of the Christian ideas we were exposed to. In chronicling the events in the life of Rev. Kit Benson, I feel I have been inspired to write of the need for a reawakening to the Holy Spirit and of the need for a return to the roots of our religious beliefs.

PREFACE

Combining my own research and study into the scriptures and historical Christianity with personal experiences with healing, dreams and visions, I think this book will raise readers' consciousness and open them up to new ideas. It is very contemporary and reflects some of the issues facing mainline churches today; namely, how do you present the Gospel in engaging and inviting ways? As a minister, do you continue the status quo? Or do you allow yourself and your congregation to be reawakened to a deeper communion with God? I take the reader along as the Reverend Benson struggles with these questions and finally finds the strength to follow the leading of the Spirit.

Ervin E. Grant

CONTENTS

1	The Seeker	1
2	The Dream	9
3	The Journey	21
4	Taking Stock	29
5	The Death Sentence	33
6	The Challenge	37
7	The Ministerial Alliance	41
8	Bible Study	47
9	The Healer	51
10	The Counseling Session	57
11	The Early Church	63
12	The Discussion Group	73
13	The New Member	79
14	Memorial Service	83
15	The Crisis	87
16	More Dreams	95
17	Blowing Our Minds	99
18	Angels	103
19	A Time of Testing	107
20	The Trial	113
21	The Kingdom of God	123
22	The Final Decision	129
23	The Final Sermon	131

1

The Seeker

THE REVEREND KIT BENSON was about to reach a turning point in his life as minister of the First United Methodist Church of Galilee, Missouri.

It wasn't as if he planned to chart a new course. After all, his friend and helpful critic Herb Miller had said to him only last week, "Reverend, if it ain't broke, don't try to fix it." This meant, he supposed, that he would be expected to follow the course suggested at seminary, and not rock the boat of religious complacency in the community.

Kit found himself imprisoned in the parsonage study, as he so often was at this point in the week, hoping for an inspiration that could be developed into a meaningful message for next Sunday's sermon. He felt vaguely uneasy about his role as a minister and pastor. He believed his wife, Jean, shared his feelings of inadequacy, but he was reluctant to discuss it with her except in a general way, because he sensed that she was not entirely happy as a preacher's wife.

"Jean, I try to be a caring pastor but I can't help feeling that my best is not good enough to make a difference in the lives of my congregation. I've been told that I am a good pulpit man, but I sometimes feel like I've exhausted all my best ideas for sermons. How can I challenge church members to feel the Holy Spirit moving within them instead of merely enjoying a weekly communal hymn sing and covered dish dinner?"

Since Jean appeared preoccupied with composing the minutes of last week's circle meeting and did not offer a response, Kit returned to his search for a viable sermon topic.

"What do you think would happen if I were to preach a series of sermons on Jesus' disciples —
each Sunday do an in-depth study of a disciple and challenge the congregation to try to emulate them?" Kit asked.

"Do you really think you could find enough in the Gospels to fill up a Sunday sermon on each apostle?" responded Jean. Without waiting for a reply, she suggested, "Why not explain the Myers-Briggs personality index and let individuals in the congregation ponder whether they are an ESTP or an INTJ? That would get them to thinking."

While Kit was considering the novelty of this approach, his train of throught was interrupted by a phone call from Hester Wilkins who wanted him to pray for the healing of her sciatica. He tried to be reasurring to her but felt compelled to refer her to Dr. Graves, a physician of good reputation in the congregation who would know much more about how to deal with such things than he did. He had not been prepared in seminary for the problems of parishioners who wanted their physical ailments to be healed by his prayers, and he felt very inadequate about this. Of course, there were the usual hospital visits and the extemporaneous prayers with the patients that things come out all right, but somewhere along the way in his preparation for the ministry, the numerous stories in the Gospels and Acts about healing had been shoved aside as irrelevant or as legends of early church experiences.

Just as he returned to grapple with Jean's suggestion that he do a clandestine personality study of his congregation in the guise of a sermon, he remembered one he had given about a year ago which had been exceptionally well received. Its theme was about the need to be born again. It wouldn't be exactly new, but perhaps if he made some cosmetic changes in it, no one would remember hearing it. Besides, it was already Friday night and something had to be ready to deliver on Sunday morning. He had just remembered that Saturday was ball practice for the men's church league and Saturday evening was the annual church bazaar; there would be little time to compose a new sermon. He was interrupted again by a phone call from Gene Hazlett, chairman of the finance committee, alerting him to the fact that the all-member financial drive was not going well and that the church was behind where it was a year ago in its total pledges. He thought that something needed to be said from the pulpit about giving more money to the church. This was an annual ritual that had to be endured, and Gene was sure to want to say a few words about how miserly most of the membership was and how a few families always pledged a majority of the budget. Gene was sometimes bombastic and probably turned off more members than he turned on, but he must be indulged for the sake of expediency, and besides this would take up probably ten minutes — Gene was not known for his conciseness of throught — and so would cut down on the time he would need to devote to sermonizing.

Just at this point and before he could make the adjustments to last year's sermon, there was a knock at the parsonage door; Liddy Harshman was ushered into his study by Jean. Liddy appeared upset and Kit sensed that another crisis was looming in the church. Skipping the usual amenities, Liddy came right to the point; "I think the devil is trying to get his claws into our 'Free Spirit' Sunday school class," she blurted out.

"Tell me what happened."

"Well," she said, "you know this New Age book that came out a few years ago about something about miracles? Well, Shirley Graham of the 'Free Spirit' class wants to use it as a study course, and when I heard about it I told her that she couldn't."

Seeing the distressed look on the pastor's face but getting no response, she continued, "So I called the district superintendent and checked with the conference office, and they told me it has never been approved as accepted material for church study and actually is considerably suspect as being the work of the devil — well, they didn't say that, but I say that!"

"Do you really feel the book is that dangerous?" Kit asked.

"Well, Reverend, you remember the scripture that says in the end times there will be false prophets and false teachings; I think this could very well be of the devil."

"Well, perhaps we should take this to the administrative board."

"There isn't time," Liddy said. "The whole class has given me an ultimatum — if they can't study this book in the church, they will meet at their homes and do it outside the church."

Kit paused for a moment to assess the implications of this situation. One of the young married women in the "Free Spirit" class was the daughter of the largest financial contributor of the church, and another couple were the son and daughter-in-law of the chairperson of the administrative board who practically ruled the church's programs and who spoke forcefully and effectively on any matter that came up concerning the direction the church should move.

Choosing his words carefully, Kit suggested that perhaps he should talk to Shirley Graham before Sunday to see if he could get her to use some of the church-approved material in the library for their study course.

"Well, I hope you can talk some sense into her. I don't know what this generation is coming to what with this 'New Age' hysteria and all — it all started with the women's libbers, and it has got to be stopped." With that Liddy departed, leaving Kit to ponder what this all had to do with women's liberation and why it was viewed as such a threat to someone like Liddy.

Liddy Harshman was of the old school where theology was concerned. She was convinced that the best description of God was to be found in the Old Testament accounts of a vengeful sovereign who demanded complete subservience from his followers, and if you sinned you weren't going to heaven so you had best straighten up. The proper attitude toward God was "fear" — after all, didn't the Old Testament prophets require that you "fear God" if you hoped for salvation? So, in addition to preparing his sermon, the pastor had to find time to interview Shirley and see if he could defuse this latest threat to the tranquility of the Galilee church.

His opportunity to speak to Shirley Graham came to him sooner than he expected when he dropped by the church after the men's church league ball practice on Saturday. He had left at the church an article about sin that he might be able to work into tomorrow's sermon; just as he was locking his office door he almost collided head-on with Shirley, who had been looking for a book in the church library.

"Oh Rev. Benson, I didn't expect to find you here," she said breathlessly. "I was just picking up a book."

"Shirley, I'm glad to see you. I was hoping I might run into you. Have you got a minute?"

"Oh yes," she replied, "I really would like to discuss something with you if it isn't too much trouble."

So Kit unlocked the door to his study and motioned Shirley inside while he took his usual place behind his desk.

"Now," he said, "what did you want to talk to me about?"

"Well, I don't quite know how to say this, but in our Sunday school class we have been talking, and we are quite dissatisfied with the lesson aids. They seem so, I don't know, so dull."

"I'm sorry to hear that, Shirley; I was in hopes that God's word would never be considered dull."

"Now please don't get me wrong, Pastor; I'm not talking about your sermons. You always make them come alive, and I really enjoy your sermons. But the material we are supposed to choose from for Sunday school discussion is all the same; it is the same stuff I've been hearing from my childhood, and I'm looking — I mean we're looking — for something new, something exciting."

"I see," Kit said. "And what, in your opinion, would be better than what the Conference has to offer?"

"Well, our class decided that there is this new book out that is supposed to be a divinely inspired discourse written down by this woman who was an atheist, and we all felt it couldn't hurt to make it the basis of a study about how to be a better Christian. It is all about miracles and everything ..."

"I guess I can't really give you much help about a book I know nothing about, but probably we could agree on some guidelines for proper Christian study in our Sunday school, and that might help us to decide what lesson aids would be appropriate. What do you feel we should go to Sunday school for?" he asked cautiously.

There was a pause while Shirley tried to collect her thoughts. She hadn't really expected to be asked what Sunday school should be all about, and she didn't even know what others might expect out of Sunday school, only that she felt frustrated and unfulfilled, not only in Sunday school but in church.

"I don't know if I can answer that," she ventured. "I guess we go to Sunday school just like we go to church, to learn more about the Bible and what Jesus taught. Maybe it's just me, but I guess I'm personally seeking something, and I'm just not finding it. I hear the same old things over and over that I've heard from my youth, while what I really want to know is what is the Holy Spirit, and what is evil, and how do I lead a more spiritual life? I think a lot of my generation are asking these kinds of questions, and we're not getting any answers in the church."

Kit was beginning to feel distinctly uncomfortable, and yet he didn't really know why. He saw an opportunity here to lead an intelligent, sensitive young woman into the light of God's salvation, but he didn't really know if he could provide any solutions that would be meaningful to her. And what was more distressing, he was sometimes bothered by some of the same feelings himself. He found himself thinking about his sermon for Sunday and whether it would be challenging enough for young people who were looking for answers in their lives.

"Kit," she addressed him by his first name, which was more familiar than she had ever done before, "Did I say something wrong? You look upset."

"No, no — you're perfectly right to be asking such questions. I guess I just got lost in my thoughts there for a moment." Then, realizing that he must bring this discussion to a close with some kind of a solution, he cleared his throat and began in his most pastor-like manner: "Let's get back to the guidelines. The Conference produces these lesson aids because it is well known that the layman needs help in interpreting the word of God; men and women who have been trained in it and have studied the Bible thoroughly try to lay down some rules as to what principles should be emphasized in the Christian life, and they assist us in formulating our own personal theology. We need to recognize our need for such advice, and especially since we bear a heavy responsibility to our fellow man not to lead him astray and not to follow false doctrines. Do you want me to have Liddy send for some study-guides so you and your class can look them over?"

Shirley felt betrayed and misunderstood. She didn't quite know how to terminate the conversation without showing her disappointment in Rev. Benson. Yet she didn't want to offend him.

"No, I guess our class will just have to go back to the drawing boards and decide what to do. I had hoped you could come up with a way to fill our needs."

She arose to go and mumbled something about being sorry to take up his valuable time.

"I am sorry I haven't been more helpful. Perhaps your class can see fit to make use of some of the excellent study aids available," Kit said as Shirley beat a hasty retreat out the door.

He sat stunned for a moment. This certainly wasn't how he had hoped the conversation would turn out. He would probably be hearing from Shirley's father, a large contributor to missions and one of the pillars of the church. "I wonder why these young people can't be satisfied with the word of God without finding some contemporary authors who will distort it into something more palatable to them," he mused. Just then the phone rang. It was Jean with news that the chairperson of the commission on missions had just passed away.

2

The Dream

SOMETHING ELSE was to happen that would be the beginning of a change in Kit's life as a minister and in his life as a Christian. It was the dream he had on Saturday night.

Now the Reverend Kit Benson had never given much thought to dreams. On occasion he would awaken in the night with the realization that what seemed so illogical yet so real was only a dream. Usually it was with a great deal of relief that some bizarre situation was not really happening to him, and on more than one occasion it had actually taken a few moments of reflection and a trip to the bathroom to calm his mind and assure him that all was normal and that no new disaster had befallen him. But he was also aware that the religion section of the bookstores in Columbus and St. Jo were flooded with new books by religious authors saying one's dreams were important and could be equated with the dreams and visions of the Old and New Testament accounts. What was disturbing to him was that if you got some kind of message in a dream, it could hardly be the result of reasoned judgment or be tested by moral principles or benefits of experience. So he was perplexed by the clarity of a dream that he could recall upon awakening, but couldn't understand.

"What's wrong, honey?" asked Jean, who had been awakened by his restlessness.

"I had a dream and I can't make any sense out of it," he mumbled, trying to clear his mind.

"Well, don't worry about it — it was just a dream. You'd better get some sleep; after all, it is Sunday morning."

But try as he might, he could not get back to sleep, and as thoughts of his partly memorized sermon-to-be kept going through his mind, he couldn't help feeling that his dream was trying to tell him he was missing something. There was that vague, illogical feeling that something was wrong in his attitude toward his flock at the Galilee church, and yet he had no clear idea what it was or what to do about it.

Seven o'clock arrived all too soon, and Kit felt he must relate his dream to Jean in hopes that she, with her greater powers of intuition, might be able to interpret it for him.

"Tell me what you make of this." he began at breakfast. "I was in a small boat drifting on a lake or small body of water. I kept hearing someone calling to me for help, but I seemed frozen and unable to help, and besides, I couldn't see anyone and didn't even know who I was supposed to help anyway. I don't know how long this went on before I felt something scraping the bottom of the boat and found I had drifted ashore. It was dark and misty, but as I stepped from the boat I saw a figure lying on the shore, and without even approaching the figure, I knew it was Shirley Graham."

Kit paused as if there were no more to say, and Jean waited expectantly.

"Yes, go on, what else happened?" she said.

"Well, that is all I can recall, but for some reason I dreamed that a little later I was in this large room — like the interior of an old castle, and three robed figures were interrogating me about something I had done. I had the helpless feeling that I couldn't think of anything I could have done to offend them but that I was guilty of something nevertheless."

"I can't make much sense out of that unless you are worried about what the congregation thinks of you — and I certainly hope it is not a bad omen for Shirley Graham. She hasn't had anything bad happen to her lately, has she?"

Kit did not want to disclose his conversation of the day before with Shirley so he merely replied, "Not that I know of."

It was a sunny, warm day, and this meant there would probably be a good attendance at church. Vacations hadn't started yet, and the choir programs weren't yet terminated for the summer so the parents of the youth choirs would be there to savor their children's performances. There was no dramatic drop in church membership or attendance, and yet he had noticed by comparison with the last two years that both membership and attendance were steadily dropping. The administrative board had considered this problem, and various reasons were advanced for the drop — all the way from major league baseball on TV to the church's continual haranguing the congregation for money. Kit personally felt it was just a sign of the times. All the churches he knew of were losing both membership and attendance, except the church with a new name and a new approach and the young minister he had heard about in the valley. They were saying it had a contemporary service on Sunday mornings with an instrumental group and even interpretive dance. He had been warned not to pay any attention to them by Gene Hazlett who had a nephew who attended there.

The Sunday morning service began pretty much as scheduled with only a few pitfalls. The public address system had a glitch in it that nobody but the custodian could seem to analyze; after he was located and directed toward the problem, it worked perfectly for the rest of the service.

The pianist, Melissa Millspaugh, was struggling gamely with a cold and managed to avoid sneezing during the hymns. By the time scheduled for the sermon to begin, the Reverend Benson had sufficiently settled his anxiety; he launched out on the morning discourse precisely at the appointed time of 11:15.

"Good morning, ladies and gentlemen," he began, as he always did. "I want to speak to you this morning about the importance of salvation. The scripture lesson is John, Chapter 3, verses 1 through 8":

> *Now there was a Pharisee named Nicodemus, a leader of the Jews. He came to Jesus by night and said to him, 'Rabbi, we know that you are a teacher who has come fromGod, for no one can do these signs that you do apart from the presence of God.' Jesus answered him, 'Very truly I tell you, no one can see the kingdom of God without being born from above.' Nicodemus said to him, 'How can anyone be born after having grown old? Can one enter a second time into the mother's womb and be born?' Jesus answered, 'Very truly I tell you, no one can enter the kingdom of God without being born of water and spirit. What is born of the flesh is flesh, and what is born of the spirit is spirit. Do not be astonished that I said to you, 'You must be born from above.' The wind blows where it chooses and you hear the sound of it, but you do not know where it comes from or where it goes. So it is with everyone who is born of the spirit.' Nicodemus said to him: 'How can these things be?' Jesus answered him. Are you a teacher of Israel and yet you do not understand these things?*

"Here we find Jesus confronting a religious leader of his day, Kit continued. Nicodemus came by night because he was a Pharisee, one of the ruling religious hierarchy. He was a pious Jew who did not want to be seen consorting with Jesus and yet he wanted to talk to Jesus secretly, and what did he talk about? Did he ask Jesus any questions? No. He didn't come to Jesus and ask, 'How do I achieve salvation?' And the reason he didn't is clear — he thought the good religious Jew already **had** salvation. After all, if one followed the ritual, kept the law and prayed to God, what more could one do to achieve salvation? So he wasn't asking for anything — he was simply giving Jesus credit for being, as he supposed, a prophet come from God. He said, 'We know that you are a teacher who has come from God, for no one can do these signs that you do apart from the presence of God.' This was purely a statement of fact. I really think Nicodemus wanted to give Jesus an opening to speak up and say, 'Yes, I am only a prophet and I don't pretend to be anything more.' If Jesus would just do this, you see, Nicodemus could go back to the Sanhedrin and report that this new teacher was another prophet of God, and since the Jews had many prophets and usually let them speak their prophecies without hindrance, that might solve this whole upheaval that was building up in Jerusalem over this Jesus of Nazareth. But Jesus was not going to shirk his responsibility. He was not about to play the role of just another prophet. Jesus saw the opportunity to tell the Jews where they had gone wrong in their religion. Here was his opportunity to tell a representative of the Jerusalem ruling class just where they fell short of piety. He had earlier referred to them as whited sepulchures and now he had his chance to tell them why.

"So he used a homely example, as he always did in his teaching. He used the most fundamental and understandable example that any human could comprehend, that of being born. He said, 'If you want to be a part of the kingdom of God you must be born again!'

At this point in his sermon, having let his voice rise to a crescendo, Kit paused for dramatic effect and looked at his congregation. Liddy Harshman was nodding her emphatic assent. Melissa Milspaugh was thumbing through the hymnal and blowing her nose, and he couldn't tell if she was listening or not. Gene Hazlett was sitting back, arm over the back of the pew, his head tilted backward and his eyes closed. He often wondered at times like this whether Gene was really conscious or was absorbed in drinking in his sermon. It didn't do any good to ask him later what he thought of the sermon since Gene's response always was, "I enjoyed the sermon, Reverend, enjoyed it."

He must move on to make his point.

"You see, being born of the flesh or being baptized with water wasn't enough if you were just going along with the law of Moses, handed down over generations and codified into neat little rules of conduct. Jesus was saying that the kingdom of God requires more than this — that there must be an inner transformation so basic that it could only be compared to being born again. And it was obvious that Nicodemus didn't understand this because he asked, 'How can a person enter into his mother's womb a second time and be born?' Nicodemus just didn't get the point! His mind was so full of ritual and rationality that all he could see was how bizarre it would be to try to change oneself so fundamentally as to be born again. He proposed to go right ahead being a good Pharisee but as far as being born again, this was a foolish idea. And Jesus, the great teacher and the Son of God, couldn't get through to Nicodemus, but his words come down through history to *us*; they have influenced kings and nations, changed societies, and been an inspiration to countless millions. The key to salvation is you must be born again."

The nod of approval from a number of members of the congregation should have been a clue to the Reverend Benson that he had reached the climax of his sermon and that any more would be anti-climactic; nevertheless, he couldn't resist adding a few words that he had scribbled on his sermon notes for the benefit of Liddy Harshman and Shirley Graham. So he plunged on.

"The impact of this timeless message for us today is that we may seek new ways of saying these words of Jesus, we may seek after those who would lead us in new interpretations of God's holy word as recorded in scripture, but we can't change the fundamental teaching — to be saved we must do the will of God. We mustn't go off on tangents trying to satisfy our curiosity or look for some emotional 'high' or feel-good form of religion. Our Christian religion is based upon fear of God and devotion to his commandments. And when he tells us we must be born again, it means we must go back to the basics of our faith and live them out in our daily lives. Salvation is within the reach of each of us if we but maintain the faith and follow the teachings of the Bible."

At this point Kit began to notice a certain restlessness in his congregation. It was approaching 11:50, and the pastor-parish committee had on at least two occasions warned him that he must plan the service so that the congregation was out by 11:45. Their reason for this was because the best restaurant in Galilee, Missouri — which incidentally was owned by the donor of the church organ — would be inundated by hungry churchgoers seeking sustenance, and the First Baptist Church of Galilee never dismissed until straight up 12:00 so that would give the Methodists an edge and a guarantee that if anyone had to stand in line to eat, it would be the Baptists.

"So we must be born again," he repeated and then bowed for a short prayer. The final hymn was rendered in only one verse in the interest of time, and soon the pastor was greeting his flock at the door as they left the sanctuary.

"Oh, Rev. Benson, I just loved your sermon," gushed Bessie Wilson, the teacher of the Cheer-up Band Sunday School Class for the last seven years. It made me feel so good to know that I am saved, and I feel sorry for those folks at the Gospel Temple down in the valley. I'm afraid they'll never get to heaven if they dance in the aisles and get so emotional. I only wish they could have heard your sermon."

"Enjoyed the sermon, Kit!" exclaimed Fred Findley, chairman of the staff-parish committee. "It just justifies the committee's faith in you on our recent evaluation. I want you to know that the committee voted to a man" — he paused, realizing that there were women on the committee, too — "to recommend to the district superintendent that you be assigned back to this church again."

Of course, Kit, who had been struggling with feelings of inadequacy and had been concerned, perhaps unnecessarily, with whether his congregation was approving of him, was relieved.

"Thank you, Fred. It's nice to know the committee feels that way." Kit couldn't help but wonder what Jiles Graham, father of Shirley Graham, would say today about his approval rating. Jiles was vice-chairman of the staff-parish committee. He looked around for Shirley Graham, but she hadn't come out of the church, and he couldn't remember seeing her today. She certainly hadn't been sitting in her usual pew.

Finally Margaret Scribner approached him with outstretched hand. She had hung back so as to be the last one out, and he knew by the look on her face that she had something important to say to him.

"Rev. Benson, I got a lot out of your sermon, but I couldn't help thinking about a controversy I read about in the Russian Orthodox Church at the time the Communists were coming to power in Russia. They had a big argument over whether to extend two fingers or three as they gave the sign of the cross while the Bolshevik Revolution was steadily undermining all that the church stood for. You could have used that in your sermon today." What could he say but, "Thank you, and yes, that would have been a good addition."

Later, at home with Jean, he was going through his weekly

transition from the "high" of the morning sermon to the drained feeling that it was over again for another week, and he felt he had given it his all. "What did you think of the sermon?" he ventured to Jean, to see if she would give her usual constructive criticism. There was a long pause before Jean began quietly, "I liked the context of it, but I wonder if anyone came away wondering **how** one can be born again," she said.

"Well, I don't know that I have the training to show anyone **how** to be born again," he countered. "After all, nowhere in the passage I quoted from John did Jesus give specific instructions on how one should be born again."

"Perhaps, but I have been having trouble with the general attitude I see in this church that they are all saved and don't see the need to think any new thoughts. Aren't they kind of like Nicodemus, who wasn't looking for salvation because he thought he had it?"

This was turning out to be different from what Kit was expecting from his wife, who usually pointed out the strong points in his sermons and remained silent if she was lukewarm or didn't approve. It raised again that uncomfortable feeling he was having that all was not well and that he was failing in his mission as pastor of his church.

"I suppose it boils down to what Jesus meant by being 'born of the spirit,'" he paused before continuing. "I have never understood his reference to the wind blowing. Does that mean that because you can hear the wind but can't see it, so the Holy Spirit is something you can't quantify — you can't use reason and logic to arrive at a state of being spiritual? And if that is true then how **do** you arrive at salvation?"

Jean looked thoughtful. "You're the one who has seminary training. Didn't they ever explain this at seminary?"

Although he had never thought of this, it now added to his feelings of confusion and doubt about what he had been trying to say in his sermon. He really couldn't think of any specific discussions among his instructors or classmates at seminary on this question of what was the Holy Spirit and how does it manifest itself. Once or twice he remembered a question being raised about it, particularly when the Book of Acts was studied. But his seminary instructor had brushed over the spiritual references in Acts with the observation that spiritual happenings may have occurred in New Testament times but that today we have the teachings of the church, and we are not under pressure of persecution as the early followers of Jesus were. This seemed to make sense at the time, but now he was confronted with people in his congregation like Hester Wilkins who apparently felt he could exert some kind of spiritual pressure on her physical problems or Shirley Graham who obviously was wanting spiritual nurturing from him.

Jean interrupted his train of thought, "I have been experiencing some remarkable images recently," she said, "and I hope you will understand if I share some of them with you."

"Images, what do you mean?"

"Well, I can't explain it, but I have been reading about it, and I have been meeting with Debbie Miller who seems to be able to draw out my images, and I have had some very unusual experiences."

Since she stopped and seemed hesitant about whether to go on, Kit quickly assured her that he would not make fun of her or criticize her. He had always shared intimate thoughts with Jean, although he sometimes wondered if she shared equally with him. But there had been no secrets between them, and he respected her common sense viewpoints on things and frequently used some of her shared wisdom in his sermons but rarely gave her any credit for it.

"I have started writing down some of my images, and it just occurred to me that some of what I have experienced in images has a relation to this question of what is the Holy Spirit."

"By all means, read some of them to me," Kit said.

"Well, at first I had trouble making any sense out of it at all," she said. "I would relax like they tell you to and try to arrive at a meditative state, and not much would happen. But lately it has begun to make sense to me, and I can't help but think that God or Jesus is sending a message to me."

"You used the word 'meditative state.' Isn't this something that people in cults fall into when led by their guru?"

"Well, really, Kit, you can't be that narrow-minded. The fact that cults may believe in meditation doesn't mean all meditation is wrong."

"No, but many people feel that visions induced by meditation may be an open invitation to the ...," he didn't want to say Satanic forces, "evil spirits to take over their lives."

"I simply don't believe that. But if you would rather not hear about my images, then that's fine."

But Kit assured her that he was vitally interested in her images and urged her to go on with her explanation of them.

"Well, I was a little girl walking along a small path with beautiful scenery all around. I was accompanied by someone I knew as the 'wise one' who was guiding me. As we came to a fork in the road, the wise one waited to see which way I would go — one way led to a beautiful shining city over a hill and another led into a deep forest. But then the image faded away, and I can't make any sense out of it. Do you suppose I was the little girl?" she asked Kit. "And if so, who was the 'wise one'?"

Kit did not presume to suppose that the wise one in the dream was himself, but he secretly wished Jean had suggested it.

"Why don't you keep a record of your images and perhaps others will come?" he suggested, as he and Jean turned out the lights to close a busy day.

3

The Journey

BY MIDNIGHT, Kit was still wide awake and deeply troubled. It was not just that he felt his last sermon had been very inadequate. It was a combination of that and the encounter with Shirley Graham and Jean's images. All of these gave him the distinct impression that God was trying to send him a message. Yet he had no idea what the message might be; he had never had these feelings of inadequacy. It had been quite a sacrifice for him and Jean to go to seminary, and yet, with the seminary training behind him, he had not experienced that great thrill of accomplishment, that sense of urgency that he had always expected a successful clergyman should feel. Life seemed so ordinary, and the problems of his church members seemed so insignificant to him. Every day there seemed to be new challenges that he was not meeting. He really wondered how much longer the congregation of Galilee Church would keep him as pastor. But even more disturbing was the thought that perhaps the congregation of Galilee Methodist Church was typical and that wherever he might be assigned in the future, there would be this same feeling of inadequacy — of not being able to connect with his people — or with his God.

He wasn't really aware of dozing off, but suddenly he was intensely aware of a presence in the room. He distinctly heard his name spoken. "Kit Benson," said the voice, "are you growing in the faith?" Kit could not see anyone, but there seemed to be a light in one corner of the bedroom. It didn't seem to occur to him that this might be unusual or that the light might awaken his sleeping wife.

"How do I grow in my faith? Pray tell me — if you know, then tell me — if you don't know then go away and leave me alone."

"Come, let me take you on a journey and show you many things that will help you grow," said the voice. Before Kit could agree or refuse, he felt himself lifted up and floating in a manner he had never experienced before. He seemed to be weightless and free-spirited, and his sense of time and urgency was cast aside. It was an exhilarating experience which seemed to be caused by the wishes of the presence he had spoken to. He could see a little more clearly now that this person appeared a little shorter than he and was dressed in a robe or tunic covering the entire body. Kit could not tell whether this person was male or female; the voice, while deep and virile, was also soothing and comforting.

"Who are you?" Kit finally got up the courage to ask.

"I am the spirit of truth — one who is sent to help you understand all things," said the presence.

"Where do you come from?" countered Kit.

"I come from a different level of consciousness. I am but one of legions of those who have gone before. I have lived a life just as you are doing, and I have suffered death just as you will. But through the death experience I have had revealed to me all things, and I am commissioned to reveal these things to you that you may impart them to your fellow Christians. Come, let me show you how it all began."

"But what do I call you, do you have a name?"

"You may call me Messenger," came the reply.

Kit began to realize that he was no longer confined to space-time, which he labored in every day, but that he was being liberated for some higher purpose which apparently had something to do with educating him beyond seminary. He at first thought of fighting against this intruder into his life, but the experience was so peaceful and pleasurable that he just relaxed and let the stranger lead him wherever he was to go.

Suddenly they seemed to be at the end of their journey, and Kit began to experience a small room with many people sitting around its perimeter on the floor. He and Messenger had come to rest in the midst of them. Kit was vaguely aware that these people were all dressed much like Messenger, and there were apparently men, women, and children of all ages. They seemed to be in someone's home rather than a church, and none of the people in the room seemed to be aware of the presence of Kit and Messenger. They began a sort of chanting or singing, all on one note, and Kit recognized a few words in Greek with which he was familiar. One elderly gentleman was chanting in English, so Kit was able to make out what he was saying. "Great Messiah Jesus, come to us again, and let us see your presence. Take us with you so that we may rejoin our fathers. Give us strength to withstand the evil one, and grant us peace in thy kingdom." This was repeated over and over again in the same sing-song chant, and because each was speaking in a different language the room was filled with unintelligible babbling.

"Who are these people?" Kit whispered to Messenger.

"These are the followers of Jesus who have just been visited by the Comforter. It has been only a little more than fifty days since Passover, and each of these people has seen the risen Christ and has been renewed by the coming of the Holy Spirit. As your Bible tells you, the Spirit struck them like tongues of fire. They are able to carry Jesus' message to other people in other provinces because each has been given the ability to speak another language. Since you are English-speaking, you understood in

English, even though the speaker had never been exposed to nor learned English. This is what the people of your day refer to as 'speaking in tongues.' But the true miracle is that they were not meant to speak unintelligibly to themselves but were to carry the message to each nation of the expanding world. So what your church members are doing is merely celebrating this great event of spreading Christ's word."

"But my congregation does not believe in speaking in tongues," began Kit. He paused when he realized that a young boy was being carried on a litter by two of the group who placed him on the earthen floor in front of one who seemed to be in a position of authority. This person was sitting near the center of the room facing away from Kit, and Kit could not determine any physical features. The room had been lit only with candles, but suddenly Kit sensed a certain excitement in the room. It began to be bathed in light, which seemed to come through an opening in the ceiling. The figure in the center of the room stood up and turned to face Kit and Messenger; Kit could now see the features of a young and graceful woman who seemed to be a leader of the group. Her face, caught in the light from above, startled Kit as he had never seen such serenity and power as she exhibited. She deftly placed one hand upon the boy's head and raised the other toward the light.

"Jesus, son of Yahweh" — Kit strained to hear — "send your healing light upon Joshua. Work your power upon any unnatural forces present within him, and lift him into the light of your Holy Presence so that your will may be done and he may be made whole." With that she took her finger and with some kind of oil anointed the boy's forehead, making the sign of a cross. Quietly, the group began either singing or chanting, Kit could not tell which, but there was an ethereal quality about it which Kit likened to the sound of a great cathedral choir. It filled the room with a great sense of joy. Some of those in the room fell on their faces, some raised their hands to the light as if in prayer, and some swayed as if intoxicated with the sound and captivated by the brilliant light which by now was focused in a beam upon the boy.

"Praise God and in the name of Jesus of Nazareth, arise and go in peace and health," cried the young woman, as everyone's attention centered on the boy. All this time he appeared to be unconscious of all that was going on, but suddenly he stirred, opened his eyes, and sat upright in the center of the group. He looked up, raised his hands, and cried out "Praise Jesus, the son of the living God — I am made whole."

Kit could not believe that such healings could be practiced by the followers of Jesus and especially led by a woman! He was so full of questions that he turned to Messenger to find out whether all this was truly happening, but he discovered that Messenger was no longer there — not by his side or even in the room. Before he could become concerned about this, there was a loud banging at the door and a gruff voice calling out, "Are any followers of the Galilean here?"

The banging at the door continued, but a change was coming over Kit. The room and the people in it were gone, and now he was struggling to clear his mind and trying to summon his reasoning powers to help him make sense of what was happening.

"Honey, I believe someone is at the door." The voice was Jean's, but the reality didn't fit with what he had just experienced. Nevertheless, he found himself climbing out of his own bed, pulling on his robe, and going to the door of the parsonage to see who could be disturbing him at this hour of night. Kit quickly glanced at his watch; it read 2:08, which couldn't be true since he had no remembrance of going to bed! When he got to the door and turned on the porch light, there was Lester Wilkins looking at him with pleading eyes and shuffling from one foot to another.

"I'm terribly sorry to disturb you so late, Reverend, but Hester has had a relapse, and we took her to the hospital. She asked if you could come."

Kit's mind was clearing now, and he realized he had just been awakened from a dream — or was it a vision? It had all seemed so real, and he had actually *been* there ...

"Can you come? I know it is asking a lot, but she asked you to pray over her before the operation."

"Of course, Lester, just let me get dressed, and I'll meet you at the hospital."

On his way to the hospital, Kit kept going over in his mind the vivid images he had encountered in his dreams — had these been sent to him to try to help him understand what this Christianity was all about? It would make the Christian religion so much more meaningful, he thought, if, indeed, the challenge issued by Jesus in the Gospels was true — that each follower of his would be granted the power to do the great works he was doing — yes, even greater works were promised to his followers after the coming of the Comforter. And he had actually been there to see this scripture in action. But now he was standing before the closed door of Hester Wilkins' hospital room, which had a big "No Admittance" sign on it.

"Come on in, Kit," Lester Wilkins urged. Kit entered with the feeling of awe and helplessness that he always felt at times of crisis like this.

"Hello, Hester, how are you doing?" he mummered, not knowing anything better to say.

"Oh, Rev. Benson, I am so glad you came. I told Lester not to disturb you, but then I guess I kind of came unglued when they told me I might have to have an emergency operation."

"Well, what is the prognosis? Have they told you any differently?" asked Kit.

"No, they took a bunch of tests and gave me a shot for pain, and I have felt a little better, but I still am glad you're here. Would you pray for me?"

A feeling of slow paralysis crept over Kit. He had been asked this question many times during his ministry, and on only one or two occasions had he really failed to find words of comfort or felt that he had not met the challenge of the moment. But now the vision of the young woman healing the boy put Hester's request in a new and difficult perspective. He wasn't sure whether Hester Wilkins was expecting him to actually heal her, or was she just wanting his words of assurance and comfort that everything would be all right.

The next words he found himself saying startled even himself, "Hester, do you want to be made whole?"

"Oh yes, yes — pray that I be healed and get well, Reverend. I know about all those people Jesus healed in the Bible, and I know he can heal me."

There was no one in the room but Hester, Lester and himself. The door was closed, so Kit placed his hand on Hester's forehead and began in a sort of stream of consciousness manner to pray over Hester. The words came easier than they had ever come before, and Kit was not sure whether it was he who was originating them or if thoughts were being put in his head and he were simply channeling those thoughts to Hester Wilkins.

"Almighty God, who through your Son Jesus showed us that health and wholeness are not accidents of good luck but are a part of your plan, we know that you desire health and wholeness for Hester, your faithful servant. We lift her up into your healing light. Enter the cells of her body and heal any sickness or infirmity that exists there that she may be free of pain and made well in body and soul. Come, Jesus, and enter into Hester Wilkins, and heal her and give her peace."

Later Kit remembered that he had left rather abruptly after praying over Hester. The nurse came in, and he felt anything more he would say would be redundant, so he accepted the profuse thanks of Hester and her husband and found his way back to the parsonage. He couldn't remember anything that happened on the way home from the hospital, and he almost felt that this prayer session with Hester had been a dream also, but the greatest need he felt right now was to get to bed and hopefully get a few hours sleep.

4

Taking Stock

THE REVEREND KIT BENSON did something he was not accustomed to doing. He stopped in the middle of his busy schedule to take stock of what was happening to him. It had been three weeks since his dream of returning with Messenger to the days of the early church, and just a week ago Hester Wilkins had called to thank him for healing her. It seems her doctor took some more tests after the night he had gone to the hospital to pray with her, and the doctor had concluded that he would not have to operate after all. In fact, the doctor reported that all signs of her sciatica had disappeared, and he had declared her to be in good health. This had come as a traumatic experience for Kit, who for the first time really believed that prayer for physical healing was possible; indeed, it had actually happened!

But he had been troubled by the Shirley Graham situation. He had learned quite by chance that there was a reason why he hadn't seen Shirley at church since his conversation with her in his study. The rumor was that she had been attending the Harbor Light Gospel Church in the valley and had been participating in the contemporary services by dancing in the aisles. This information did not come from Shirley, of course, nor from any of the Graham family but was dutifully reported by Liddy Harshman, who seemed almost gleeful that the problem of the proper Sunday school curriculum had been solved and God had prevailed over Satan.

Although he hadn't discussed this with Jean, it was evident that she knew all about it.

"Do you know what Debbie Miller told me yesterday?" she asked when they were finally able to spend some time alone after the morning church service. "She said Shirley Graham and Martha Hobson and Bob and a couple of others from their Sunday school class had been to the Harbor Light Church and seem to like it very much."

Kit tried to keep his composure since he realized his wife hadn't known about his conversation with Shirley or her desire to study new material.

"I wonder why those young people would go to another church when they were brought up in our church and their parents go here?" Jean continued, since Kit had made no response.

"Maybe the young people are seeking something and are not finding it in our church," Kit said absently. "I think too often the youth want excitement and new experiences that we don't seem to be able to give them."

"That's interesting," Jean mused. "I wonder why the Christian religion can't be exciting and vital as it apparently was with the disciples right after Pentecost?"

Kit didn't reply, but an idea was germinating in his mind for next Sunday's sermon — that is, if he dared to preach on such a controversial subject.

"Did I tell you I had an interesting series of images yesterday while I was meditating — and this was without Debbie even being around to encourage me?" Jean asked.

"No, what was your image this time?"

"Well, it was real strange and I certainly don't understand it, but it was so vivid I can remember it very well. It seems I was out in the mountains and walking along this narrow path and all of a sudden I was observing myself. I had a little cloud around me, and I could see an umbilical cord going from my body back along the path as far as I could see. I could sense myself going back in time and I saw my parents and my grandparents, but I sensed that I went back much further in time than this, and a voice said to me: 'That's just the way it is; before you were born you were with God,' and I knew that my spirit was connected to God and always would be."

Kit found himself strangely moved by this account of Jean's images and at a loss for words. When he was able to recover he simply said, "That's amazing."

"I don't know what to make of it because it almost sounds like reincarnation, and yet I have never taken that seriously. But it does give one a new perspective to believe that you are connected to God and always have been, even since before you were born."

"Yes," said Kit, "and it gives meaning to Jesus' words to Nicodemus that you must be born again. Too bad I couldn't use your image in a sermon, but I'm afraid I'd be hooted out of church."

"Well, maybe your sermons should educate our church members about the way Christianity started out — how vital and alive the disciples were and how they were able to heal and to experience the Holy Spirit!" Jean was now expressing the very same thoughts he had been struggling with for weeks, and he could hardly believe that he and his wife could both be feeling the same frustrations at the same point in time when neither of them had really had any in-depth discussions of the matter.

"I will have to admit to you that there is apparently more to this thing of being a Christian than I was able to learn at the seminary," he began, and then he related his experience with Messenger in his dream and his prayer with Hester Wilkins that seemed to heal her.

5

The Death Sentence

IT HAD BEEN a difficult sermon to prepare, and Kit knew it would be a controversial one to deliver in view of the fact that the state legislature was struggling with a bill to allow the death penalty. The latest state-wide poll showed some 60 percent of the voters favored a death penalty for certain types of murder. But on this Sunday morning in the Galilee Methodist Church, he knew the time had come to make his plea to the congregation for something he strongly believed in — the death penalty was wrong and was contrary to God's plan for us.

"I want to discuss with you this morning something that I know many of you have set opinions about, but please hear me with an open mind today, for I sincerely believe that our Lord and Savior spoke eloquently to this recurring moral problem that our society seems to struggle with periodically. I refer, of course, to the efforts to reinstate the death penalty in our state. It is easy enough to say 'an eye for an eye and a tooth for a tooth and a life for a life' without stopping to realize that this is only a cop-out — a reference back to Old Testament times long before Jesus, when civilization was in its infancy and the Prince of Peace had not yet appeared on the scene with his message of love and forgiveness. When Jesus appears, he pronounces a message which was certainly controversial for his time but is still controversial for our time: love your enemies, do good to those who despitefully use you, turn the other cheek. To the thief on the cross he said, 'This day you will be with me in Paradise.' He did not say, 'But you have committed a crime against society so I should condemn you instead of helping you.' He did not say, 'I will help you if you make restitution and do penance and go into a monastery.' He simply said, 'This day you shall be with me in Paradise.'

"Both Jesus and the thief were looking beyond their predicament of the moment. Jesus was suffering because the society of his day considered him an enemy. The thief was suffering because of his crimes against society, but both were more concerned with a new life in a new existence. Both believed there was an after-life that was more important than this life. Both were being judged by society, rightly or wrongly. Both believed that this life is only an introduction to the next. It seems to me that if we could really understand that, we would not be so quick to try to judge others in this life. We would leave the matter of judging to God. After all, he plainly said, 'Judge not lest you be judged.' "

At this point in the sermon, Kit noticed Bruce Bongard slip out of his pew and leave the sanctuary by the side door. Gene Hazlett had not assumed his usual disengaged position and was learning forward in his pew, frowning. Liddy Harshman appeared to be receptive, but Fred Findley was flushed and obviously troubled, and Kit wondered if Fred were preparing to have a heart attack. Even so, he felt compelled to go on with his sermon:

"It seems to me there are two human reactions that occur when the state is carrying out the death penalty. One is the group of demonstrators who carry signs and call insults to the accused and who cheer and celebrate with a bonfire at the moment the prisoner's life is taken — much like a rally before a football game. The other group lights candles and sings hymns in a silent vigil that expresses a loving, caring concern for all human life. In which group do you put yourself?"

By this time in the sermon the appointed closing time had arrived and none too soon, as Kit was painfully aware that at least a dozen of his faithful parishioners had left their seats and removed themselves from the sanctuary. Kit really couldn't recall later the closing hymn or the benediction, but he sensed a certain tension among those who shook his hand at the door.

"I am sorry, but I don't agree that the death penalty is that bad," mumbled Vince Packard, the football coach. "I guess it makes a difference if you've known someone well who was brutally murdered."

"This certainly wasn't your best sermon, Reverend," said Bessie Wilson. "It made me very uncomfortable, and I don't come to church to be made uncomfortable or to be preached at."

There were a few who congratulated him for taking on a controversial topic and three or four who actually expressed their agreement, but Bruce Bongard, Fred Findlay and Gene Hazlett had taken the very extraordinary step of slipping out the side door to avoid him. Neither Shirley Graham nor her father Jiles seemed to be in attendance, and Kit had a let-down feeling as he closed the sanctuary doors. He turned to secure the sanctuary and to find Jean to inquire what she thought of it all.

"Reverend, I believe you used the wrong scripture this morning," came a voice from the back of the sanctuary, and Kit discovered it was Fred Findlay, who apparently had thought better of his hasty departure and had returned to the empty sanctuary to confront Kit.

"Oh," said Kit, "what scripture should I have used, Fred?"

"You should have quoted Exodus 21: 12: 'Whoever strikes a person mortally shall be put to death.' It's right there in the Bible, Reverend, and you can't say the scriptures don't support the death penalty."

"Fred, I hope I didn't upset or offend anyone. I was expressing my personal opinion, and I realize others feel differently. But as far as your scripture, I think you will find that the very next verse says, 'Whoever strikes father or mother shall be put to death.' You will also find, 'Whoever does any work on the Sabbath day shall be put to death.' You see, Fred, these instructions are found in the Old Testament; when Jesus came along he changed all these harsh rules of the Jews and said, 'You shall love your enemies,' 'You shall turn the other cheek.' When they were about to stone to death the prostitute, because Jewish law required that she be put to death, Jesus said, 'Let him among you who is without sin cast the first stone.'"

Fred seemed to have no ready answer to this so he turned abruptly and walked away, leaving Kit to wonder if he had been too hard on Fred.

The Challenge

MONDAYS were the pastor's day of rest according to the custom of the Galilee church. Since Sunday was Kit's busiest day of the week, it was only right that Monday would be his day off, but Kit frequently found that things intruded on his free time. More than once he had remarked to Jean that he wondered if God was disturbed by someone's troubles when after six days of creating everything, he took a well-deserved rest.

Kit was not enjoying his Monday of rest because he kept worrying why he had chosen to speak on such a controversial subject just at a time when it was important to keep the good will of his parishioners. The Methodist Church used a system of appointing ministers to local churches, and Kit had served the Galilee church for five years; whereas the average time a pastor remained in a local church was about six or seven years. Besides, the same old doubts kept flooding back into his mind — the Shirley Graham situation, his dream and Jean's images; he knew he had probably alienated some important church members. Why couldn't people keep open minds about their religious beliefs as they did about business and politics? But then, he was not sure how open-minded they were about those, either.

Just as Kit was considering a round of golf to clear his head, there was a knock at the parsonage door. Bruce Bongard made his appearance looking decidedly uncomfortable. Kit had not become well acquainted with Bruce Bongard and was somewhat surprised to find Bruce wanting to talk to him, especially since he thought the militia was on a bivouac this time of year. In fact, Kit blurted out, "I thought your militia was on maneuvers, Bruce."

"No, that isn't until next month, Reverend. But I've been delegated to see if you would do something to start up a Bible study class in our church."

Kit had to suppress a smile at Bruce's customary, no-nonsense, get-to-the point approach, but sometimes it was refreshing to find people who did not spend a lot of time getting to the issue they were interested in.

"I guess I wasn't aware there was that much interest in a Bible study class," said Kit. "How many do you think would be interested?" he asked, as both men settled comfortably into the living room chairs."

"Well, I know of five or six, but if we let it be known I'll bet we could get at least a dozen," said Bruce.

Kit was not sure what to say to this, as he was completely unprepared for such a request, especially from someone like Bruce Bongard. Kit considered Bruce an arch-conservative in political viewpoint but had never had any discussions with him about his religious views. Yet Kit recalled that Bruce was one of those who only yesterday had left the sanctuary during his sermon on the death penalty. Now here he was, strangely suggesting that Kit lead a Bible study.

"There is an interesting Bible study course available — the 'Disciple' series that is a different approach to Bible study," said Kit, but then remembering who he was talking to, Kit added, "but it might not be structured enough for some, although it is definitely recommended by the conference office as the proper way to do Bible study."

"I don't know about that, but some of us definitely feel that we're not following the word of God in our lives anymore and that we need to get back to the Bible."

Kit pondered what this was supposed to mean. He hadn't known Bruce well, and Bruce had always seemed distant and hard to relate to. He attended church fairly regularly, but Kit had heard that Bruce was a captain or a lieutenant in the militia outfit that really had no relation to the army or the National Guard but was apparently a group of self-appointed men who felt the government was becoming too obtrusive and that law enforcement was part of their problem. Kit had never actually been afraid of Bruce, but he wondered what kind of philosophy the group believed in and whether any other of his church members were in Bruce's militia.

"Can you tell me who else from our church is interested in this?" asked Kit.

"Well, of our church only Wesley Sowers and Carl Green, but I know of a couple of guys outside our church who feel strongly about this."

"And what about women — are there any wives that are interested?"

"We don't want the women involved in this, Reverend. They already have their circles and study groups. We want this just for the men."

Kit considered in his mind whether it would be politic of him to suggest that excluding women might put them afoul of civil rights laws, but in view of Bruce's reputation he thought better of it and so only responded "umm."

"At least, why can't we pick a week-night and get out invitations and see how many we could get organized?" asked Bruce.

Kit felt the implications of the word "organized" might not bode well for the success of the type of Bible study he had in mind, so in order to placate Bruce Bongard and try to gain himself some time, he came up with a suggestion: "I'll tell you, why don't you get your group of five or six together and I'll be glad to meet with you some evening this week or next, and let's just bat around some ideas of what the group wants before we invite anyone else."

"That sounds fine with me, Reverend. Any night of the week is fine except we have militia military drill on Tuesday nights. I'll call the church secretary and work out a night next week."

"Fine," said Kit, who was glad to have something decided and who suddenly realized how tense his muscles had been throughout the conversation. When Bruce had left, he remarked to Jean that of all the things that might have come up on Monday, that was certainly the least expected.

7

The Ministerial Alliance

GALILEE wasn't a large community, but it did have five churches — if one disregarded the Harbor Light Gospel Church in the valley. There was one Catholic Church, a Lutheran, a Baptist, an Assembly of God, and Kit's Methodist Church. At least every three months the pastors of four of the five got together to compare notes and share problems. Kit looked forward to these "ministerial alliance" meetings, and he especially enjoyed dialogue with the young Catholic priest from St. James. The differences in technique in their pastoral care of their parishes did not seem to weaken a great common bond between them of genuine concern that they were meeting the needs of their congregations.

"I am concerned that the average person does not take the Christian religion very seriously," Kit confided in Father John as the four of them gathered for one of their informal get-togethers. "They seem to feel that the church's sole reason for being is to help them approach God or to shield them from God's wrath."

"Then, I take it, you don't agree with that?" asked Jim Burke, the Baptist minister.

"No," replied Kit, "I think the church's role is to assist them in realizing that God wants to reach out to them. We spend so much time worrying about how we can entice them to the Sunday morning service and how we can meet the budget of the church and not much time trying to find out what their needs are — what's happening in their daily lives and how we can help them interact with the Holy Spirit."

"I agree with you," said Father John. I expect my parishioners to attend Mass regularly and I will hear their confessionals, but I keep feeling that something is missing in our mission to them; we are not reaching them with our ritual and our catechism. There has to be something more, perhaps something the early church had that we've lost along the way. I am hopeful that in our church we can begin to meet this need using a spiritual director on a regular basis."

"A spiritual director?" asked Kit. "I know each of us does a certain amount of counseling, but I am not sure what you mean by a spiritual director."

"Starting next month we have employed on a part-time basis, a person who will be available to the congregation — not as a priest or to hear confessions — but to interact on a one-to-one basis with those individuals who want to receive assistance from someone who will direct them to God."

"That's exciting," said Kit. "Tell me more about this. Where did you get the idea and how were you able to fill that position?"

Before Father John could explain, Rev. Burke, who had been listening intently and shifting in his chair, raised his hand as if to stop the conversation before it left the realm of theology and entered the realm of psychology. "Wait a minute," he said. "I can't agree with your premise that we aren't doing right by our congregations. I feel I fulfill their needs by educating their minds out of God's Holy Bible and warning them against following sinful ways. This is what Christian churches have traditionally done, and it is what Jesus told us to do. Besides, I am not sure whether most people know what the Holy Spirit is — I am not sure *I* know what it is — and if you bring a 'spiritual director' on board, are you not going to have competition between the priest or pastor and this director?"

"Competition for what — for gaining a convert for Christ?" asked Father John.

"Well, yes, and competition for the loyalty of the congregation. It is important that they learn the word of God from one reliable source; what if the pastor and this 'spiritual director' disagree on their theology?"

"Ah, I'm afraid you're putting too much emphasis on what kind of dogma you can provide them and are too concerned that someone might cause them to think for themselves, and this might challenge your position," rejoined Father John.

"No, I continually try to get them to think about what the Bible says. I spend most of my time appealing to their thought processes, and besides, you should be the last one to talk about imposing dogma on your congregation!"

Father John managed a bemused smile at this outburst by his Baptist friend since they frequently differed on their theological viewpoints; they remained the best of friends even though they always had very frank discussions at these get-togethers.

"Well, I've been trying to get a word in edgewise in this discussion, and I tend to agree with Jim here that if you're concerned with giving them only dogma, then you need to be telling your Pope to quit issuing encyclicals and papal bulls. And as for the fact that we've gotten away from the practices of the early church, I suppose all of us have guilt in our background because of the excesses of the Crusades and the Inquisition and some of the cardinals and popes who weren't quite what we would regard as Christian in hindsight," added George Cross, the Lutheran minister. "We certainly aren't any of us perfect, and we don't help things by being critical of how the past history of our particular denomination developed."

"But the theology should not be different for a Catholic or a

Methodist or a Lutheran or a Baptist. We all believe that we are human and therefore sinners and that our job is to try to get right with our God; Jesus and the Scriptures told us how to do that, and we need to believe and practice our faith and not go off on tangents that aren't in the Bible," pronounced Jim. "The fact that I'm a Baptist doesn't mean I will have any better chance to get to heaven than you guys will, but we won't any of us get there if we depart from God's word in our preaching."

This brought a laugh from all present, and the discussion might have ended there except that Kit still had not had his question addressed.

"But I still want to know, John, where you got the idea of a spiritual director, and how did you find one? And does your church organization condone this type of position?"

"The Catholic Church is actually in the process of training spiritual directors. I don't know whether they are authorized from the Vatican for individual churches but our Synod approves them, and the more charismatic of our dioceses are trying to bring them in. We don't feel they should be a threat to our priests or bishops because the effort is to try to assist each individual to have a personal experience with God or Jesus, and if this is sometimes referred to as the Holy Spirit, then so much the better."

"But the individual church member can know God personally through the lessons given to us by Jesus, and we know his parables and examples of right living that he embodied. I think we tend to over-emotionalism when we feel we have to have the spirit move us in order to be good Christians," said Jim.

"Well," responded Father John, " let me give you an example of what I'm talking about. We recently had a young man in our congregation commit suicide. He was active in our youth group, and I had known for a long time that he was having problems; I even tried to counsel him but he would never come to me individually for counseling nor for confession. I learned in a roundabout way that he was being sexually and emotionally abused — I am not at liberty to say by whom — and he was really looking for something in his religious life that he wasn't finding in the rituals and practices of the church. He attended mass fairly regularly but seemed very dissatisfied. We will never know whether he used suicide as a way out of what he considered a hopeless situation or whether he so yearned for a spiritual life that he thought he could find it in heaven if he could just get there.

"But how would having a spiritual director have saved him?" asked Jim Burke.

"We can't be sure it would have, but we know he was intensely interested in finding someone he felt he could relate to so he could unburden his soul to them. He apparently felt I was too tied to the church hierarchy to fulfill that role. He was continually reading about the mystical religions of the East and even considered entering a monastery. He was turned down by the monastic order, and he couldn't get any of the civil authorities to believe him about the sexual molestation. I guess he took the only way out that he knew."

There was a long pause. Each pastor thought about how this tragedy could have been averted. "Fortunately, we haven't had that type of problem in our congregation," muttered Jim. "We keep them so busy they don't have time to think about sex or drugs, and we have lots of social activities where they can relate to their peers. If they show signs of backsliding, we have a special Bible study class in which we heavily emphasize that they are human and easily influenced and that the devil is always looking for a convert."

"In other words, you either shame them or scare them to death," suggested Kit with a broad smile. "Come on, Jim, give them a break. Don't they have minds of their own, and can't they reason or doubt or experiment without it being the devil that's after them?"

"I think your young man was just weak," said Rev. Cross. "Our job is to build up their strength in God and teach them by example and right living. If they are too weak, they should be shown the way to earn their salvation, and if they can't do that, then they will fall by the wayside."

"I think we owe them more than that," insisted Kit. "And if they show an interest in the so-called 'mystical religions,' we should encourage that. We know that Jesus told us that the only way to the Father was through him, and yet I believe Hindus and Buddhists and even Muslims believe in one God; their particular religious leader is a prophet or personification of that God, so why doesn't it follow that all religions are on parallel tracks to the same destination, which is salvation with God?"

"Oh, I can't accept that, Kit!" exclaimed Jim Burke, "and I don't really believe you do either. I think you are putting us on. It is very clear in the Bible that Jesus is the only son of the true God and that we will be enticed by false leaders and false doctrines, especially in the end times, but we must resist them because only the true believers will be saved."

"Now Jim is going to lecture us again about the rapture and how his 144,000 Baptists are the only ones who will be taken up to heaven," laughed Father John.

Since Rev. Cross had to leave for another appointment, the meeting adjourned amidst a good-natured disagreement over how to achieve salvation, with an understanding that the discussion would be renewed at another time.

Bible Study

THE NIGHT FINALLY ARRIVED for those interested in Bible study to meet, and Bruce Bongard had convinced eight men to come to the meeting strictly on an experimental basis. The parlor of the church seemed the proper place to get together, and Kit was surprised to see that only three of the eight in attendance were familiar to him. He felt this should not interfere with the plans since once it got started, word of mouth or invitations in the bulletin would probably attract more of the congregation.

After welcoming the men and asking each to introduce himself, Kit planned to ask some questions about what they were expecting to learn from the study and then explain the "Disciple" plan of study that was based upon study books and a series of meetings extending over thirty-six weeks. There was a Catholic, two Episcopalians, a Lutheran, and a person who professed no church affiliation. Kit suspected that at least three of the group were fellow members with Bruce in the militia, but he wasn't sure.

"What type of Bible study would you like?" began Kit. "One method is to go straight through the Bible trying to pick out passages that you can use to apply to problems in your daily lives and perhaps memorizing those passages. Another method is to use approved Bible commentary to study each chapter and verse of the Bible to see how biblical scholars have interpreted it. The Methodist Church has come up with a third way — what is called "Disciple" Bible Study — where selected passages are studied over thirty-six weeks covering about eighty percent of the material in the Bible. This approach is from the standpoint of 'what is this passage saying to me?' This is a method in which the leader does not impose certain beliefs on you but seeks to find out how each person responds to a certain biblical teaching and then the group discusses those responses."

Kit paused, hoping to get some sign of what the group wanted.

"Reverend, I don't want anybody interpreting the word of God to me," said Bruce Bongard. "I want to know what God said in the Bible so I can judge what is right and what is wrong. I don't think enough people study the Bible; if more of us did, I don't believe we would put up with all these drugs and killings that are going on. I think we need to listen to God's word and live by it."

"Yes, and it really bothers me when we talk about interpretations and discussing what the Bible means. You are supposed to tell us what it means because, after all, it is God's word," responded one of Bruce's friends.

The Catholic in the group objected to using any translation but the King James Version and believed that any other version was "man's manipulation of God's work."

The two of the group who were members of Kit's congregation other than Bruce Bongard expressed interest in trying the "Disciple" series, but Kit could see that this was a very diverse group and that a majority probably expected him to dictate to them what they should believe.

"One of you mentioned that I, as leader of the study, should tell you what the words of the Bible mean. Would not that mean I am interpreting the Bible?" asked Kit.

"You know what I mean, Preacher, I just don't know how to put it in words. Everybody knows that God wrote the Bible and it is God's word and we need to accept it and get others to accept it. But that means you have to tell us because when I try to read the Bible there's some of it I don't understand," said the Lutheran.

"And how do you know that when I tell you it means a certain thing, how do you know I am right?" asked Kit.

At this point the Catholic in the group spoke up. "I have been trained since I was a kid in what the Catholic Church believes and I already know what the Bible says. I don't need anyone to tell me — even my priest doesn't do that. What I need is how to apply what I already know to life's daily situations."

"Yes, that is what we need," said a number of those in the group.

Finally the group disbursed after assuring Kit that they wanted to use only the King James Version, and they wanted to bring to the group personal examples of acquaintances of theirs who they knew were not practicing what the Bible teaches. Kit was to help them know how to go to such acquaintances and straighten them out by passing on the true word of God. When the last member left, Kit was suddenly aware how cold it was in the church parlor, and he felt as if all of the vitality had been drained out of him and was replaced by a sense of foreboding about the future of the class. How could he possibly pull together such a diverse group who already had their own preconceived ideas about what the Bible said and were really looking for an opportunity to use Kit to proselytize their neighbors who were mired in sin?

Kit turned out the lights and sat for a moment in silence while a feeling of intense emotion flooded over him. He found himself saying aloud, "Lord, help me to have the insight and the courage to do your will with these, your children. Help me to be able to open their hearts to your true message and to put aside their petty prejudices and preconceptions. And, above all, Lord, let me be able to keep them from destroying themselves."

It was a longer than usual walk home as Kit seemed to walk with a troubled gait. When he arrived at the parsonage and opened the door, Jean was immediately aware that all was not well. "What's the matter, honey? You look beat. And where's the car — didn't you drive it home?"

9

The Healer

KIT HAD KNOWN since he was a child that some of the healings in the scriptures spoke of the "laying on of hands," but he had always assumed this was symbolic or perhaps a custom of those practicing healing in those days. But that was before he met Duane Taylor. The occasion of their meeting was a request from Milicent Fenway to use the chapel of the church for a healing seminar which was to feature Duane as the healer.

"And just what is it you do to accomplish this healing?" Kit asked Duane in the church office when the request was presented to him.

"I only do God's will," Duane replied. "It is really rather simple. It has to do with the natural magnetism that exists in all of us. We are all like a magnet with a positive and negative pole — just like the earth — and electromagnetic waves flow from our positive pole to our negative pole. This has been known for centuries; in fact, the originator of chiropractic healed by using electromagnetism as early as 1895, but medical science has pretty well overlooked this source of healing."

"Do you use a machine, then, to create the electromagnetism, or how do you administer it to cure the sick?" asked Kit.

"No, it is all a natural process. Anyone can do it; it does not require special training or equipment. It involves controlling the flow of the magnetic forces in the body. For example — if one has a pain in the hip, I hold my left hand over the area — not touching the hip but holding my hand a few inches away from it. This serves to draw out the forces causing the discomfort. This may be how the early disciples were able to heal by laying their hands on the afflicted, and Jesus certainly approved because he sent them out and commissioned them to heal in his name."

"How do we know this works?" asked Kit. "I have to get the permission of my administrative board to allow holding of such sessions in the church, and they are going to ask me what proof we have that this heals people and what scientific principles are at work here."

"As far as scientific principles, they are the same ones that control the compass and that are responsible for the seasons. As far as scientific proof that this works, I can only cite examples. We don't know exactly why working with the magnetic field of the body should relieve pain and cure illness, but I can give you a number of personal examples of cases where healings occurred," responded Duane.

"By all means, do so," urged Kit.

"Well, first of all there is the woman who called me from the hospital. She was diagnosed as having a malignant tumor in her breast. They had established its malignancy by biopsy and were to operate to surgically remove the breast in a few days. I simply controlled the magnetic flow around her body and treated her this way on two occasions at her request but without the sanction of her doctor. When the time came to perform the surgery, the tumor had practically disappeared and surgery wasn't necessary. Her doctor couldn't understand it, and when she finally told him about my treatment, he called me in and asked how it happened."

"I see," said Kit. "Go on."

"Another case was the little boy who was diagnosed as having myotubular myopathy. This is fatal in 98 percent of cases, and such children don't usually live but a few days after birth; the doctors only gave the parents about one chance in twenty that the child would survive. This baby was not able to make any sound, even when it cried, and no one could understand this. I treated the child for a few times in the hospital, and after the parents took him home I taught them how to treat him at home. This child is alive today, and many signs of his disease have disappeared; he is beginning to make baby sounds and cry in a normal way."

Getting no response from Kit, Duane continued, "Then there are a number of people who have simply had bad headaches or pains in their legs or bad colds, and they have felt fine a few hours after a treatment."

Kit was uncertain what else he should ask and unsure just what his administrative board would think of this, so he paused to see what Duane Taylor would say next.

"As far as I am concerned, I never begin a treatment without a prayer, and I feel I am simply using the natural forces of God to bring about in people the wholeness that God wants them to have, as expressed many times in the Bible."

"If this is so effective, why hasn't it been used more, and why doesn't the American Medical Association promote it?" asked Kit.

"It hasn't been used more because we are so brainwashed to believe that chemicals or surgery are the answers to all illnesses; that we have no control over our own ailments and are actually encouraged to believe that we can't get well unless the doctor is controlling our lives. Sometimes we are taught that we don't really want to be well. After all, if we could be healed in these simple ways the surgeons, the oncologists and the specialists would suffer a significant reduction in income and wouldn't have the control over our lives that they have now."

Kit could envision this presentation being made to the ad board of his church. There would be Dr. Graves, a general practitioner who was chairman of the board, and Lucille Erickson, a registered nurse who was also a member. Lester Wilkins was a retired pharmacist, but Hester's recent cure of her sciatica might make him more receptive to this new method of healing than he would have been before.

"I think I am obligated to have you make these remarks before the members of the ad board at this next meeting because church policy says that if a seminar is to be held by someone coming in from outside the congregation, they must put their stamp of approval on it," said Kit.

So Duane Taylor was invited to the next ad board meeting. He had to sit through the reports of the various committees and the lengthy report of the trustees. This took longer than usual because Carl Hawes, chairman of the trustees, had to educate everyone present about the cracks appearing in the foundation of the parsonage and the shut-down of the main boiler, which had survived its annual inspection; only later had the building committee found that the boiler was completely worn out and would have to be replaced, probably before next winter.

"This evening we are to hear a few remarks from Mr. Duane Taylor who has requested the use of the chapel to put on a seminar on healing, and you all know that we have to give approval in cases like this," began Dr. Graves, when the subject was finally reached on the agenda. "Mr. Taylor, the floor is yours."

Duane Taylor began with some of the same statements he had made to Kit, but after relating the healings of the patient at the hospital and of the infant, he was interrupted by Chairman Graves, "Are you saying that you are able to heal people by laying on of hands?" asked Dr. Graves.

"No, sir, I don't do the healing, God does the healing; I am simply saying that by the natural process of controlling the electromagnetic field around the body, healing has been proved to occur."

"Can you cite me any clinical studies by reputable members of the medical profession that support your statement?" asked Dr. Graves.

"No, sir, I can only cite Dr. Larry Dossey who has proved that prayer contributes to healing, and I incorporate prayer in my treatment, but I don't think the medical profession has taken a position on this means of treatment," replied Duane.

"Well, I'm sure they haven't either, anymore than they've approved Ouija boards to make diagnoses. You mention that Egyptians used to use this method of treating diseases and I say, yes, we in the medical profession at one time used to 'bleed' patients or apply poultices or do other mumbo-jumbo, but we learned that it didn't work. We applied the scientific method and in controlled double-blind experiments we could prove what was effective and what wasn't; we've moved beyond the primitive medicine men that we once were. I, for one, don't want to go back to that."

There was a long, awkward pause. Kit was considering in his own mind how he might pour oil on the waters to defuse a tense situation, but before he could intervene, Duane responded to Dr. Graves' statements.

"Well, sir, the medical community have adopted a typical head-in-the sand attitude and are not willing to consider God's natural healing laws because once they admitted that a person could invoke God's laws to heal themselves, then the pill-pushers and the surgeons and the pharmacists would be out of business. The AMA really doesn't want to see anybody cured; it is in their best interest that we all stay sick so that they can make money off of us. I question whether we are really trying very hard to find a cure for cancer, because if we ever do, the oncologists and the hospitals and the suppliers of radiation machines will all be unemployed. It is time we wake up and see what is happening to us."

Kit observed the flushed face of Dr. Graves and the look of horror on the face of nurse Erickson.

"We will discuss this matter privately and let you know," said Dr. Graves. "The meeting is adjourned."

Many days were to pass before Dr. Graves would even speak to Kit about the request for a healing seminar, but Kit knew that if Duane Taylor were to hold his seminar it would be elsewhere than in the chapel of the Galilee church. Kit privately hoped that Milicent Fenway would find another place for the seminary so that Duane Taylor would have a chance to prove his technique on any church members who might attend. Kit was somewhat skeptical of Duane's claims for healing, but he was willing to be proved wrong.

10

The Counseling Session

ONE OF THE THINGS Kit enjoyed most about the ministry was the occasional opportunity to do pastoral counseling. Although he had little formal training, he felt he had a somewhat natural empathy for other people's problems and an ability to listen well. But his abilities were never more sorely challenged than the day Edith Frazier asked him to meet with her and a friend from another denomination who was having problems.

"Pastor, I want you to meet my friend Alice. Alice, this is Rev. Benson," began Edith as all three gathered in the church office. "I have become well acquainted with Alice from our support group for abused women, and since Alice belongs to another church in this community, she has been very reluctant to get help, but today I have convinced her that you would be willing to talk to her and that you might be able to help her."

"Of course, Alice, I am glad to meet you, and I am certainly willing to listen to you and provide any help that I can."

"Thank you, Reverend. I really don't know how to begin. I know I shouldn't have come here, but Edith convinced me it might be all right."

There was a long pause during which Kit fully expected Alice to think better of her decision to seek counseling and to terminate the session, but he waited to see if she would explain her problem.

"Reverend, will anybody know that I have been here? Will any word get back to my church?"

"Well, certainly, I won't disclose any confidences and I'm sure Edith won't, so no, there is no way anything you say here will leave this room," said Kit. "And, by the way, please call me Kit."

"Do you want me to leave the two of you alone to talk?" volunteered Edith.

"No, no, please don't go, I can't even begin unless you stay."

Kit could detect signs of panic in Alice as she said this. He estimated she was about 35, but she was restless and considerably unsure of herself.

"To begin with, why don't you tell me a little bit about yourself?" began Kit.

Okay, I'm a teacher at Archer Elementary School, and I live with my parents on a farm just north of town. My father is the pastor of the New Life Assembly Church here in town, and he has been there going on eight years."

Alice paused and looked down at her lap. Kit prompted her with another question.

"Are you comfortable with your church?"

"No, that's just it, Reverend, I'm so miserable I could just die."

Alice began sobbing. Edith tried to comfort her, and Kit produced the box of Kleenex he reserved for just such situations. When she was able to go on, Alice apologized profusely and offered to end the session.

"Sometimes a good cry is a catharsis for the soul and helps us see our situation in a better light," Kit reassured her. "Can you tell me what there is about your church that's troubling you?" he asked.

"Well, I don't know how to explain it or what to do about it, but some of the things my father says from the pulpit make no sense to me. He gets up every Sunday and lambasts every other church in town. He tells us their churches are filled with people who are alive, all right, but their churches are dead. He says their preachers are misguided because they don't preach the Gospel; they don't interpret the Bible right. He would be horrified to know I am here talking to you because he says nobody should go to this Methodist Church and that none of you are going to heaven."

At this, Kit stole a quick glance at Edith Frazier, but she was looking only at Alice with deep compassion and sympathy.

"... and I never can be good enough," continued Alice. "I try and try to please my parents and please God, but they always point out to me where I have fallen short. I go to church to learn that I just will never measure up to their expectations, and no matter how hard I try I never get the feeling that I am loved or that anyone cares about me."

The pent-up anger and frustration were now cascading out of Alice, and she seemed to take advantage of this opportunity to unburden her soul. "But that's not the worse thing — what really bothers me is that my parents talk one way during church service on Sunday but just the opposite once they get home from church. They preach that we should honor God and they preach love and human kindness to your fellow man, but they are so judgmental and show no understanding at all. I can't remember when they ever showed that they loved me; they are always criticizing everything I do and telling me if I don't straighten up I'll never get to heaven."

Alice abruptly stopped talking and began silently sobbing to herself.

"Have you considered trying to get some counseling to help you understand why they act this way?" asked Kit.

"Oh, I wouldn't dare, Reverend. If I ever left the church

they'd kill me or at least shun me, and I know I wouldn't go to heaven. And as to why they act that way, I already know that; we are brought up that way. Nobody ever admits he has done wrong; it's everyone outside the church who is always wrong. They have all the answers and they're saved, but people like me aren't good enough to go to heaven."

"And what do your church members believe God is like?" asked Kit.

"They don't believe he is forgiving. God doesn't love us, he just judges us. He isn't someone we can go to to get help; we just have to please him and follow his commandments. Jesus doesn't love you if you sin."

Kit was becoming so angry that his hands were shaking. He wanted to lash out at the hypocrisy of it all, but he realized that wouldn't provide the help Alice was looking for.

"Didn't I hear you say you were in some kind of support group?" asked Kit.

"Yes," responded Edith, "she has been coming to an abused women's support group sponsored by the Order of St. John, and I think she is getting some help there, aren't you, Alice?"

"Yes, it is really helpful to find that there are people who care and will listen to your problems. I like the support group, but I have never told my parents or anyone in our church that I go there. They wouldn't approve."

Kit felt Alice needed some reassurance. "Self-esteem is very important to our spiritual health, and if it has been repressed for much of our lives, it can be hard to develop it, but I would certainly recommend that we work on that, and I would welcome you to come back as often as you feel comfortable so we can talk again," he said. "In the meantime, please continue to attend the support group as I am sure you will find others there who are struggling with the same problems."

After a short word of prayer, Alice arose to go. She did not look directly at Kit but confided that she found it helpful to talk out her feelings and that she was most appreciative of his help.

Kit wondered if he would ever see her again. He feared for her peace of mind if anyone in her church ever learned that she had come to him.

11

The Early Church

SERMON FOLLOWED SERMON with routine regularity and with little inspiration on Kit's part. He wasn't getting any objection from his congregation about his sermon topics, but there wasn't much favorable comment either. Usually the conversation at the church door as members were leaving on Sunday morning had to do with their health or who was visiting them or how their family was. Kit could not remember a serious discussion with any of the congregation since his confrontation with Shirley Graham. How could he bring inspiration to their lives if all that interested them was the state of their health or their pocketbook? Jiles Graham hadn't said a word to him in weeks, and Shirley had apparently left the church for good.

Kit felt relieved that his annual two-week vacation was coming up and he could seek new life outside the church for sermons, which might give the congregation a respite and give him renewed inspiration. He had in mind asking his studious friend, John Stanton, a professor at the local community college, to fill the pulpit. John had such a refreshing outlook on the history of the early church movement and could perhaps lead some of his parishioners into a new way of looking at their religious convictions. Kit always enjoyed his occasional in-depth talks with John, who was well-read and somewhat of an expert in the first three hundred years of the church's existence. The more Kit learned of the history of the early church, the more he became convinced that present-day churches had strayed from their original practices. On those occasions when Kit could get together with John Stanton, it was exciting to learn from his research just what the early church members did before centuries of history masked the efforts and beliefs of those early disciples.

From John, Kit had learned that the original "churches" established by St. Paul were a far cry from our present-day idea of a church, in that they were made up of unorganized cells of people who took turns leading the worship. The early church did not have a standardized set of scriptures as we have today. The converted Jews, of course, had the Torah, the first five books of what we now call the Old Testament. These had developed over a period of time from the sixth century B. C. to the fourth century B. C. and were the fundamental law of both conduct and faith to the Jews. However, the Gentile converts to Christianity were not familiar with it and did not feel bound by the food laws and the rites of circumcision of the Jews. The basis of faith of the early church of the first century A.D. was the personal experience many members had of Jesus' life and teaching, and this was spread outside of Palestine by word of mouth and by traditional sayings attributed to Jesus and handed down from generation to generation. Many of the new church members were exposed to the writings of the "church fathers" such as Clement and Ignatius, and, of course, the letters of Paul were circulating about Asia Minor before our present "gospels" were in existence. John Stanton believed that probably the earliest gospel writer was Mark, believed to be a disciple of Peter; both Matthew and Luke borrowed from Mark's testimony as well as from a source known today only as "Q" (from the German word Quelle, meaning source).

From John, Kit had also learned that it is believed that a

written account of the sayings of Jesus was circulating even before Mark and that this common background of the gospels, possibly being the mysterious Q source, may very well have been the writings of a group known as "gnostics." One of these accounts, which was discovered in 1945 at Nag Hamadi in Egypt and known as the "Gospel of Thomas," was apparently a collection of sayings and parables of Jesus composed possibly as early as the second half of the first century A. D., prior to Matthew and Luke and possibly prior to Mark. This account claimed to be "the secret sayings which the living Jesus spoke." These writings had been banned by the early Church, which attempted to destroy them because they were considered "heretical"; nevertheless, they may have been available as scripture for the early church members of the first century.

Kit knew from his research that some writings such as the "Didache" and First Clement" were probably written earlier than the gospels. The second century had produced many writings by the church fathers who followed after the apostles, so the early church had to choose those writings that it felt were genuine for use in worship. The book of James was regarded as scripture as early as 184 A.D., and the Apocryphal writings of the "Shepherd of Hermas" and the "Apocalypse of Peter" were early regarded as scriptural although they later were rejected from the "canon" of accepted scripture.

John had concluded from his study of the early church that by the end of the second century A.D., Iraneus, Tertulian and Origen, all early church writers and Christian apologists, were using a canon of scripture which is about the same as in use today. The earliest "canon" of scripture was referred to as the Muratorian Canon and included the Wisdom of Solomon and the Apocalypse of Peter. The Council of Carthage in 395 A.D. finally accepted the canon of scripture that we know today as the New Testament.

Kit pondered just how much of this history of the early church to incorporate into Bible study, as it probably wouldn't fit with what some of the prospective members had said they wanted. However, Gene Hazlett had indicated to Kit that he had recruited a few more members from the church congregation, so possibly a majority of the Bible study group would be open-minded enough to accept the history of how the New Testament came about.

The time to test this out on the members of the group arrived with the first scheduled session of the Bible study group. Kit was pleased to see that in addition to Bruce Bongard's earlier prospects, there were five more members from his congregation who showed up for the first meeting.

"I want to welcome you all here tonight, and by way of background to this Bible study, I would like to give you a little history of the way the Bible, as we know it, was written," Kit began. He then recounted the information he had learned from his own study and from John Stanton.

"We know that the Jews follow a tradition that the first five books of our Old Testament, which they call the 'Torah,' were all written by Moses. They believe this even though the Book of Deuteronomy gives an account of the death of Moses and what happened thereafter. So we don't really know who wrote Genesis and the following four books, nor do we know *when* they were written. But obviously it was written after the fact by someone who observed how God's creation operated and was writing his or her explanation of what he or she observed. For instance, it could be readily observed that the universe is orderly and follows a set pattern; hence, it must have been created to follow that pattern. It could be observed that human beings can choose between right and wrong; thus, there must be both evil and good forces at work in the universe. It could be observed through experience that certain actions by mankind produced beneficial results, whereas other actions produced harmful results and so there must be a creator who rewards good conduct and punishes wrong choices. The writer of Genesis could see that childbirth caused pain to the female and that the male had to struggle against nature to produce crops; thus the story of Adam and Eve — Adam representing male human creation and Eve representing female. The power of choice is represented by Eve, who was tempted by the snake to eat the forbidden apple and who then offered it to Adam when God had prohibited them from doing this; they knew what they were doing was wrong. The story of Adam and Eve being thrown out of the Garden of Eden is the writer's way of saying perfection is not available to us on this earth but that perfection does exist. We are offered a glimpse of it in this earthly life, but perhaps it is reserved for us in a heavenly existence after this life."

Kit was interrupted by Bruce Bongard. "Wait a minute, Pastor, are you trying to tell us the biblical account of Adam and Eve isn't true? That they weren't the first man and woman and the Garden of Eden didn't exist?"

"I am saying that the writer of Genesis, whoever he or she was or there may have been more than one, was writing allegorically trying to explain what they observed going on around them in the universe, just as you might do if called upon to explain how creation occurred and why we have right and wrong choices. As a matter of fact, many over the years have written a very different account of how the earth was created, and you all know that one of these accounts is a scientific explanation that says the earth was millions of years in creation and that mankind appeared on the scene fairly recently as historical time goes. This idea was, of course, severely condemned by the Church at one time because it didn't fit with the explanation given by the writer of Genesis. However, the writer of Genesis simply didn't have the scientific knowledge available to him that more modern writers do and shouldn't be faulted for writing about events in a way he can explain them."

There was a period of silence, but it was soon broken by Gene Hazlett. "But, Kit, you yourself have said that the Bible is the word of God, so wasn't Moses or whoever wrote it setting out God's explanation of events?"

"Well," said Kit, "rather than trying to answer that, I will let you decide for yourself. Since you all brought your Bibles, look at Genesis 1:20 through 27. Here it says God created fish and birds and then animals and last of all humans to have dominion over the other creatures. But if you look at Genesis 2:4 through 8, you find that before any plant life or animals existed, God created 'man' from the dust of the ground and then at 2:18 created a partner so man wouldn't be alone, and only then did God create all the animals and bring them to Adam to name them. According to this version, Eve was created last because man could not find a 'partner' in the animals. Now if God is dictating these words to Moses, which account are we to believe?"

"I think this is all heresy," said a friend of Bruce Bongard. "I was brought up to believe in the Bible, and I don't cotton to this idea of evolution and that we all sprang from monkeys. I think that's what you're trying to tell us, and I consider that very un-Christian. I suppose you don't believe God created the world in seven days either?"

"Again, instead of my trying to tell you what to believe, just use your own God-given intelligence to arrive at your own conclusions. Let me tell you that an Irish Archbishop by the name of Ussher, using the genealogical tables in Genesis to compute back to the time of creation, arrived at a date for creation of the world of 4036 B.C.; not to be outdone, the vice-chancellor of Cambridge University, who lived in the seventeenth century, decided that creation took place the week of October 18 to 24 in 4004 B.C. with Adam being created on October 23 at 9 a.m. Greenwich time. Now, in view of fossil remains of millions of years ago, we have to decide whether trying to use the Bible as a historical document is valid."

Kit paused, and there was a stunned silence, with even Bruce Bongard unable to respond to this explanation. Finally it was Gene Hazlett who responded, "But maybe God created the fossils in order to confuse us."

"Yes, there is that theory," said Kit. "Some say the fossils were placed on earth by the devil to mislead us. But I choose to think that God took his own good time to create animals and humans in a gradual manner and that the writer of Genesis was not writing *history* but was writing allegorically according to what he observed. Again, if any of you were to sit down and try to write how the world was created, without the benefit of any of our scientific knowledge and without any Bible to influence you, how would you explain it? You might receive inspiration from God — and I am certainly *not* saying that the Bible isn't the inspired word of God — but God still might not tell you all the secrets of the universe which we are not privileged to know but might inspire you to write an explanation that would make sense to an unsophisticated, uneducated person.

"I guess I had never really thought about it that way," said a friend of Bruce Bongard's.

"I find that hard to believe," said Gene, "but then again, I guess I never really thought about it either."

"Well, with that kind of open-mindedness let us discuss the first study lesson, which is about how the Bible was written and about the Pentatuch, the first five books. Did you realize before you read the study lesson that the first five books are basically the present-day Jewish Bible called the 'Torah'?"

"But, Pastor, I don't understand. How did all these diverse

writings, which must have been written over a great span of time, ever get put together into what we call the Bible?" asked one of the group.

"The church, over a period of many years, held 'councils' to decide what would be acceptable in a 'canon' of scripture, which the church officials could use as reliable sources of the word of God. These decisions, at the Council of Jamnia as far as the Old Testament scripture is concerned, and at the Council of Carthage in 395 A.D., as far as the new Testament is concerned, were man-made decisions; many writings that existed at the time were rejected by this group of self-appointed censors, so we do not know that just because writings were rejected means that they were heresy although certainly some were so labeled. The remarkable thing is that even the Gospel of Thomas, written by the gnostic group and banned by the church officials as heretical, even these writings are remarkably similar to the versions given us by Matthew, Mark and Luke, and, in fact, the gospels could have relied upon them as being earlier recorded accounts of the actions and sayings of Jesus."

"So the Bible didn't just come into being in one writing as if it were dictated by God?" asked Gene.

"No, like everything else that has worth and great value, it was the product of much labor and patient reproduction in order to give us the great Bible we have today."

Since the time for adjournment had arrived, Kit closed the meeting with prayer. Most of those attending seemed to leave with little more than a degree of confusion or dismay, but Bruce Bongard and a friend of his asked to stay to talk to Kit for a few minutes.

"Rev. Benson, I am really disappointed in this first session. Will they all be like this or do we get into the meat of what the Bible really says?" asked Bruce.

"We will take up different historical events and study what

the prophets or gospel writers recorded about them. Is that what you're looking for?" responded Kit.

"I really don't know what I expected, Reverend, but I know that what I want out of this is to be able to say to my neighbor when he wrongs me that he will be punished in the after-life, and I want to be able to cite the Bible to prove it."

"I see," said Kit. "You are saying that you really don't want to understand what the Bible is about, but you want to memorize the wording so you can threaten someone who would be what the Bible calls a sinner?"

"Well, no, I don't mean that. I want to know what it takes to live a Christian life, and I have always been told that you get that from studying the Bible. But I also want to be able to teach others when they go wrong, and I want to use the Bible as proof," responded Bruce.

"Well, I can only urge that you stay with us a few sessions and then if what I am saying doesn't make sense to you and if the Bible itself doesn't begin to speak to you, we can always terminate the study if it isn't helping you learn the Christian beliefs."

With this, Bruce and his friend left. Kit could only ponder whether all this effort was to bear any fruit and whether using "Disciple" was a wise choice for this group. Again, Kit was feeling a sense of inadequacy and concern that he was not leading the Bible study in a way that Jesus would want.

12

The Discussion Group

THE PRESSURES of the ministry were such that the Reverend Kit Benson began looking for a relief valve that he could activate when things seemed to close in on him. He finally decided on a pattern of impromptu get-togethers of a few men in the congregation whom he could easily relate to and in whom he could safely confide. It was relaxing and also edifying to meet occasionally in the basement of the parsonage to discuss topics not only of theology but also of politics and social issues. Kit had chosen carefully these select few and felt completely comfortable at their sessions. There was John Stanton, the professor at the local community college; Vince Packard, the local high school football coach; Mark Ewing, a young lawyer in the community; and frequently joining the group was Earl Redmond, the operator of the local movie theater.

At one of these unscheduled, spur-of-the-moment get-togethers, the discussion centered on a recent drug raid in the community and how so many sins of society that used to be found only in St. Louis and Kansas City were showing up in Galilee.

"Why can't things be like they used to be?" asked Vince Packard. "It used to be if a kid got caught in school it was for throwing spit balls or paper airplanes. The local youth might turn over a local farmer's out-house on Halloween, but by and large they were pretty law-abiding and they never ended up in jail. If they were disciplined at school and that got back to their parents, they were disciplined at home, too. But that seems to have all changed."

"Don't you think part of it is how much more they are exposed to nowadays?" suggested John Stanton. At age twelve, they know more and have seen more than we did at age twenty-one."

"I agree," said Kit, "and I feel the blame lies at the door of the entertainment industry and also partly at the door of each of us as parents for letting it happen. In my younger days, whenever there was a love scene in the movies the camera would pan away from the kissing couple to show a sunset or waves breaking on the shore. You could use your own imagination as to what was happening, but at least you weren't being a voyeur while the couple undressed and went through all the foreplay and actual sexual intercourse that is standard fare nowadays."

"I guess I'll have to come to the aid of the movie industry," said Earl Redmond. "I really believe you don't see that as much on the big screen as you do on TV, where it is an intrusion into our very homes; unless we're warned it's coming, it may be playing on the tube right before our kids' eyes."

"Wait a minute," interrupted Mark Ewing. "Most of what is objectionable on TV in my opinion are the replays of what has already run its course at the local theater, and as far as the ratings are concerned, they're a joke; what the Hays office used to ban on the screen would easily pass as PG13 now, and what was considered hard core pornography in my day is rated R nowadays."

"Well, there has definitely been a change in the entertainment field. The effort seems designed to appeal to the basic instincts in us rather than appeal to our high sensibilities," said Kit. "It used to be that it was not considered proper to kiss on the first date, but look at what they do now on first acquaintance."

"I think it's going to be the downfall of our civilization," replied Mark Ewing. "I am convinced that there is a force of evil behind all of this — a few people in Hollywood who want to test the rest of us and see just how far they can go before we rise up and stop them. They keep yelling about their First Amendment rights to literary expression, but they are absolutely amoral when it comes to showing any responsibility, and they want us to be that way, too. I think it is high time the churches took a stand on this."

"What would you have the church do?" asked Kit.

"I would be for having church members who were willing to picket the local theater when they show some of this garbage, and we should have a sermon on the problem at least twice a year," said Ewing.

"You won't change anybody's mind by picketing," said Redmond. "I think picketing just gains sympathy for the businessman who is being picketed."

"Isn't it basically a problem with each of us individually, rather then a collective problem?" asked Kit. "If each of us was a good Christian, do you think Hollywood would produce the kind of movies they are producing? Don't they reflect the public mores rather then create them?"

"No, sir, I do not believe for a minute that they merely reflect the public mores," said Stanton. "The reason advertisers pay thousands of dollars per minute on TV ads is because they know that they influence your behavior — in their case it is to get you to buy their product, but the effect is just as strong if it is TV violence or shaping young people's attitudes about sex."

"I notice you mentioned a force of evil, Mark," said Kit. "I would be interested to know how you would define evil. Is it a person — like the devil — or is it the absence of good or what is it?"

There was a sudden lapse in the conversation. Kit was particularly interested in discussing this because he was considering composing a sermon on the nature of evil but wondered if it would be too esoteric for this congregation. If he could tell how his parishioners felt about the subject, it might help him with his sermon.

John Stanton was the first to respond. "If you study the history of the church, you will find that the idea of Lucifer or Satan as a fallen angel is basically not biblical — it is found only in Daniel and Revelation. It actually started with St. Thomas Aquinas, and although evil is found throughout the Bible, it is usually disguised as something other than a figure of a devil — in the Garden of Eden story it is a snake, for instance. I think we need to acknowledge that evil exists in the world — after all, our God-given ability to choose between good and evil wouldn't mean much unless God had at least allowed evil to exist. But to ascribe some kind of demonic form to evil or to see evil as a devil with horns and a tail is strictly of our own creation."

"But why would God even allow evil in his creation, much less create it?" asked Mark.

"That has been the theologians' dilemma throughout the centuries," ventured Kit. "We cannot really know why evil is found here in God's creation anymore than we can understand how the stars and planets were formed. There are just some things we are not supposed to know, but maybe when we die and assume another form of consciousness, we will be shown all things and can understand."

Kit suddenly quivered. He realized that he was almost paraphrasing Messenger's statement to him of a few weeks ago. He wondered whether he should confess his dream or at least lead the discussion into the subject of dreams as messages from God. The pause in the discussion had been just long enough for two of the members to rise to go. The discussion of dreams must await for another get-together.

13

The New Member

DUANE TAYLOR was building quite a reputation — either good or bad depending upon whom you talked to. After the administrative board rejected Milicent Fenway's request that Duane be allowed to use the church chapel for his healing treatments, she succeeded in finding him an unused room offered by the local chiropractor. Some church members began seeing him regularly. Milicent Fenway herself gave eloquent testimony to his healing abilities since she no longer experienced back pain after only two treatments. She was very outspoken in her church circle about the benefits of Duane's treatments. A few other circle members had clandestinely sought him out, but a vicious rumor was finding its way into the Galilee community — that Jean Benson, the pastor's wife, was visiting this healer more often than necessary. Jean was aware of the stories being told of her visits to "the healer," and she immediately confided these rumors to Kit.

"I guess you know that the latest scandal in this town involves me and Duane Taylor," Jean volunteered one evening just after she and Kit had retired from a tiring day.

"I only know that you have explained his methods of treatment, and they seem to be helping your arthritis," responded Kit.

"Aren't you a little jealous, or at least concerned that your parishioners are saying I have a romantic interest in Duane Taylor?"

"Honey, I trust you, and if he can do anything to relieve the pain of your arthritis, I guess I'll just have to put up with the rumors," said Kit.

"I wonder if it would help squelch the rumors if Duane would join the church — he has attended a few times," suggested Jean.

"I don't know whether he could weather the animosity of Dr. Graves and some of the ad board — I actually think they are the ones who have been spreading stories about him. But the only Christian thing to do is to invite him."

"Good, I really think if the members of the church get to know him, they will accept him — all except perhaps Dr. Graves and Lucille Erickson," added Jean.

So it came about that Kit made a special visit to Duane's office to invite him to join the First Methodist Church of Galilee, and Duane accepted the invitation. But on the day he was to be admitted to membership, his letter of transfer couldn't be found, and the chairperson of evangelism took ill and could not make the presentation. Kit didn't think too much about this until two weeks later when he again scheduled a new-member reception; this time the church secretary failed to notify Duane and he didn't attend church that morning.

Kit was pondering whether all this was coincidence or design when Fred Findlay approached him after church and asked if he could talk with him for a few minutes.

"Certainly, Fred, come on in to the study and shut the door if you wish," said Kit.

"Pastor, I notice that someone has proposed Duane Taylor for membership in our church. This is very awkward for me, but I feel it is my duty to tell you that a number of members have approached me about whether he is of sufficient moral character that we would want him in our church."

"Fred, I wasn't aware that his morals had been questioned. I know he has been using a healing method that is unconventional, but I know of nothing that would prevent us from welcoming him into our church family," said Kit.

"Well, difficult as this is for me to say to you, Kit, there are rumors he is having an affair with your wife."

Kit paused, as he was not really expecting such a blunt accusation from his staff-parish chairman, but he knew his response must be handled diplomatically.

"Well, Jean and I have discussed these rumors, and she is aware of them; we felt the best way to confront them and disprove them would be to invite him into our fellowship where the congregation can get to know him better."

"You understand, Reverend, that I have the greatest respect for Jean, and I don't put any faith in these rumors, but it seems to me that to invite the very subject of the rumors to be a member would be like throwing gasoline on fire."

"Fred, I am quite disturbed that the people of this congregation would give any credence to accusations like that. Do they really think my wife is doing something wrong by taking treatments from Duane Taylor?"

There was a long pause while Fred Findley fidgeted and tried to find words to respond to Kit's question.

"It's just that it looks bad. The man is not a medical doctor and nobody believes his claims about using electricity or whatever he says he can do. It is just a suspicious situation, and I'm afraid it will get worse unless we," Fred's voice trailed off and it didn't appear he was going to complete his thought.

"Unless we what?" asked Kit. "Are you suggesting, Fred, that we condemn the man before he has a fair trial? Are we as Christians to reject him before the members of the church even get to know him? Are we all to give in to some rumors probably started by our administrative board without any Christian charity?"

"Well, I'm just chairman of staff-parish committee, but I've talked to Gertrude of the evangelism committee, and she thinks we shouldn't invite him."

"Fred, I am really concerned about this congregation. We have some very loving, spiritual people, but I keep clashing with some elements of our church that don't seem to accept my ministry of openness and love for our fellow man. I feel it is my duty as your pastor to lead individual members of the congregation into a personal experience with God, and yet I keep experiencing rejection. Do our members not feel I am bringing them the true word of God; where am I failing in my mission?"

"I have been meaning to discuss that with you, too, Kit, but now is not the time or place. Right now I think we should address the problem of Duane Taylor, and it is our recommendation that he not be invited to join the church."

"He has already been invited to join. You are telling me he should be told now that he is being shunned by a few self-appointed people who believe false rumors about him?"

"Well, I wouldn't put it that way, but I've said my piece, and you will have to decide what to do about him."

With this, Fred made a hasty exit. Kit reviewed in his mind all the things that had gone wrong lately, and he wondered where he really stood with the congregation of the Galilee Methodist Church.

14

Memorial Service

THE NEWS CAME as a blow to the community but particularly so to Kit. The newspaper reported it as the death of Alice Conroy, age 35, without giving a cause. Edith Frazier was able to provide Kit the details — how Alice had been improving with the help of both the support group and Kit's counseling sessions, but her parents had learned of Alice's efforts to escape what she called the "tyranny of their religion," and they had convened a church council to determine a proper punishment.

"And, Rev. Benson, Alice told me they forced her to get up in front of the congregation on Sunday morning and admit all that she had done — the counseling and everything. She said they claimed it was a way to purge herself of the influence of the devil, but I knew it made her situation worse. She quit coming to group, but she had promised me she would come see you again. I guess it was just too much for her to handle so she took her own life."

Kit could not think of anything to say. Why must those who profess to be acting according to Jesus' teaching so pervert the message that he brought? Kit felt a flush of anger, not just at the members of the New Life Assembly Church but at all the tragic injustices that had been done in the name of Jesus throughout the ages. How could people be so blind and so heartless? Kit thought of the legion of wise, dedicated women who were burned at the stake because of the vindictiveness of church leaders in the Middle Ages and of the needless deaths that occurred because of the Inquisition and how the victims must have felt as they faced the church leaders as their executioners. Surely God must have grieved over his children.

Kit was roused from his reverie by a question from Edith: "Rev. Benson, do you think we dare attend the funeral services at the New Life Assembly Church?"

This was something Kit had not even considered, but it was certainly a question that must be dealt with.

"I don't know how many in your support group are members of our church," responded Kit, "but I am certain that neither you, nor I, nor any of our church members would be welcome at the funeral. And yet I can't help thinking that Alice would want those who care to honor her memory to do so in some sort of service."

"Perhaps we could hold a memorial service in our church much as is sometimes done for someone who is killed in the service or lost at sea and their bodies aren't recovered," suggested Edith.

"Yes, that would be possible. Of course, it would be interpreted by her church members as further evidence that it was all the fault of us instruments of Satan and that we couldn't leave her alone, even in death."

"Well, I don't particularly care how their congregation feels about it — I just think it would be the Christian thing to do," replied Alice.

And so it came about that the Galilee United Methodist Church held a memorial service for Alice. The attendance was small, but Kit had never felt so inspired about a funeral service as he did about this one.

"We are gathered here to honor and celebrate the life of one of your faithful children, God. A life of service and seeking for your truth was cut short by the tragic misunderstanding that some of your children have adopted from your message of love. Some of your children have so surrendered their lives to forms and ceremonies devised by men that they are blind to your message of support and concern for our fellow human beings. Since we crucified your son, we have learned little — we go on crucifying in your name, believing that we are doing your will but tragically misunderstanding what your gospels are all about.

"We also know that Alice has crossed that thin dividing line between life and death. It is referred to by those who have had near-death experiences as pulling aside a curtain and passing from one side to the other. We grieve for the loss of our loved ones, but we realize that this is a selfish attitude on our part and that the person for whom we grieve is experiencing feelings of complete joy and peace. It is hard for our minds to comprehend this, but if proof is needed, we again have the many similar near-death experiences related by those case studies on the subject. If we could only bring ourselves to accept that the rewards awaiting us after death far outweigh these earthly experiences, we would have a whole new outlook. We would have the courage to come to the aid of someone in danger or the ability to forgive someone who has killed our loved one. We would also look at the funeral experience as a time of rejoicing and honoring the good things in the lives of the deceased.

"Today we honor Alice, and we thank you for her limited years of Christian service as a school teacher and friend. We know today that she is with you, where she is surrounded by complete and supporting love that she desperately needed but never found in this life. Let her life and her tragic death be a lesson for all who come after her, that as you told us, we are not to judge but only to love unconditionally. May her soul rest in peace."

As the service ended Kit noticed a solitary stranger slip out of the back pew and leave without speaking to anyone. "I tried to get Alice's mother to sit down front, but she paid no attention to me," reported the usher.

15

The Crisis

A FULL-SCALE CRISIS was developing at the Reverend Kit Benson's First United Methodist Church of Galilee, Missouri. How could Kit have known that the innocent act of inviting Professor John Stanton of the local community college to fill the pulpit would have caused such dissension among his flock and threaten his position as pastor? It had seemed a good idea at the time. John Stanton, professor of religion at the local college, had been attending services off and on for the full four years that Kit had served this parish; it was well known that Professor Stanton's views on the history of Christianity were controversial. But it was also well known that he had made the effort to be certified by the local church conference as a "lay speaker," meaning one who without the benefit of seminary training still exhibited a grasp of theology and possessed an ability to communicate ideas that qualified him for this special title. It had been the custom in the Methodist Church to call upon such lay speakers when the regular pastor was to be on vacation or when emergency situations arouse and when a minister from another church might not be available.

Kit had felt a certain dissatisfaction among his congregation even before the eventful Sunday, but he was confident that his congregation was open-minded and loyal enough that some new ideas from a different source would not offend them but perhaps would even challenge them. So he had invited Professor Stanton to address the congregation on a subject of his choosing, not bothering to screen his ideas beforehand. Since Kit had been on vacation that Sunday, he had not learned of the content of the sermon until the chairman of the administrative board had insisted he listen to the regularly recorded broadcast of the sermon shortly after his return from vacation.

Kit had known John well enough to know that he was quite a scholar on the subject of the early Christian church of the first and second centuries. He had engaged the professor on the subject of the development of the church after the Pentecost experience on a number of occasions. Kit had found these discussions tremendously interesting, and they had stimulated him to make his own study of the beginning of the Christian church. He had even given a sermon on this topic himself about a year ago without creating any excitement or inciting any adverse reactions. But Professor Stanton, when given the privilege of the pulpit, had seemingly pulled out all the stops, and now Kit had an insurgency on his hands among his parishioners.

"Just listen to this, Rev. Benson," said Gene Hazlett, as he rewound the tape to play it for Kit. "How could any good church member say things like this from the pulpit?"

The tape began with the liturgist making announcements. Then came the liturgy and hymns chosen by Liddy Harshman, who had volunteered to help John on everything but the sermon. First there was "The Old Rugged Cross" and two verses from "Give Me That Old Time Religion" before the professor approached the pulpit to read the scripture for the day.

"The scripture lesson for today is from Matthew 24:3 through 8 and Matthew 24: verses 29 through 36.

"As he sat on the Mount of Olives, the disciples come to him privately, saying, 'Tell us, when will this be, and what will be the sign of your coming and of the close of the age?' And Jesus answered them, 'Take heed that no one leads you astray, for many will come in my name, saying, 'I am the Christ' and they will lead many astray. And you will hear of wars and rumors of wars; see that you are not alarmed; for this must take place, but the end is not yet. For nation will rise against nation and kingdom against kingdom, and there will be famines and earthquakes in various places; all this is but the beginning of the sufferings.'

"For false Christs and false prophets will arise and will show great signs and wonders so as to lead astray, if possible, even the elect. Lo, I have told you beforehand. So, if they say to you, 'Lo he is in the wilderness,' do not go out. If they say, 'Lo, he is in the inner rooms,' do not believe it. For as the lightning comes from the east and shines as far as the west, so will be the coming of the son of man.

"Immediately after the tribulation of those days the sun will be darkened, and the moon will not give its light, and the stars will fall from heaven, and the powers of the heavens will be shaken; then will appear the sign of the Son of man in heaven, and then all the tribes of the earth will mourn, and they will see the Son of man coming on the clouds of heaven with power and great glory, and he will send out his angels with a loud trumpet call, and they will gather his elect from the four winds, from one end of heaven to the other. From the fig tree learn its lesson; as soon as its branch becomes tender and puts forth its leaves, you know that summer is near. So, also, when you see all these things, you know that he is near, at the very gates. Truly, I say to you, this generation will not pass away till all these things take place. Heaven and earth will pass away, but my words will not pass away. But of that day and hour no one knows, not even the angels of heaven, nor the Son, but the Father only. As were the days of Noah, so will be the coming of the Son of man. For as in those days before the flood they were eating and drinking, marrying and giving in marriage, until the day when Noah entered the ark, and they did not know until the flood came and swept them all away, so will be the coming of the Son of man. Then two men will be in the field; one is taken and one is left. Two women will be grinding at the mill, one is taken and one is left. Watch, therefore, for you do not know on what day your Lord is coming."

Kit listened with apprehension as the recorded sermon continued:

"We have almost identical words found in Mark's gospel. In point of time, Mark was written first, but Matthew and Luke apparently took their ideas from a source, since lost to civilization, that scholars label as 'Q', which must have been a collection of accounts written down by eyewitnesses or disciples of Jesus to record what he said. This type of writing, referred to as eschatology or apocalyptic writing, was typical of the Jewish expectation of the coming of a great Messiah who would destroy the enemies of the Jews and would cause the faithful Jews to arise from their graves and enter into a millennium of peace. We find such writings in the Old Testament in the Book of Daniel, as long ago as 535 B. C. But we encounter a dilemma when we find the gospels attributing such eschatological ideas to Jesus since they do not fit in well with Jesus' overall message.

"In Luke 17:20, when Jesus was asked by the Pharisee when the kingdom of God was coming, he answered: 'The Kingdom of God is not coming with things that can be observed, nor will they say — look, here it is, or there it is, for the Kingdom of God is among you.'

"So, we have a dilemma here; on the one hand, Jesus is reported as using the language of Daniel to explain that in the end times one will come as a Son of Man, on the clouds and in great glory, while at another point he is quoted as saying no one knows when the end will come, and we should not await the end or expect it. So he seems to be saying the Kingdom is already here. But an even greater dilemma is found if we compare these sayings of Jesus with the words, 'Truly I say to you, this generation will not pass away until all these things have taken place.'

"We know that the end of the world did not come within the generation of the disciples he was speaking to, and although Paul and the early apostles expected him to come during their lifetime, many generations have come and gone and the end has not come. So, was Jesus wrong? Was he mistaken? Does this mean that the good news of the gospel is not credible, or is there another explanation?

"After many years of studying the Bible and the Christian apologists and biblical critics, I have come to the conclusion that the students of the Bible are right when they say that the verses of Jesus quoting Daniel, found in all of the gospel writers but John, constitute later insertions of eschatological ideas which the Jews of those days wanted to incorporate into the gospels. The so-called 'Little Apocalypse' found in the 'Olivet Discourse' is apparently wording inserted by later writers trying to link the expectation of the Jews for a Messianic coming to the prophesies of Daniel of centuries before. The actual saying of Jesus — namely that with his coming the Kingdom of God has already arrived and exists among men and that we should not seek nor expect a great social event in history — should tell us that a 'Second Coming,' as we term it, is not biblical. God simply does not operate in that way. The Jewish disciples of Jesus' day wanted to proclaim him a king — the long-awaited Messiah, who would throw off the yoke of Rome and lead the Jews out of bondage and into an earthly kingdom of eternal peace. But he would not accept that role. So much more so, we should not expect Jesus to return again to this earth as a heavenly king, returning to gather up his faithful and destroy the wicked. But far from believing that Jesus was misled or mistaken in his references to the end of existence happening in one generation, I am convinced he was not wrong but that his ideas have been misinterpreted. I believe the so-called 'Second Coming' occurs to each one of us — and thus to each generation — at the point of our death. Jesus must have had this in mind when he said: 'Two will be in a field — one will be taken while another is left; two women will be grinding meal together — one will be taken and one will be left.' This certainly describes what happens when one drops dead and the other continues to live. It also fits with what we now know to be the scientifically verified experiences of those who have gone through the near-death experience. Almost all of those who have reported this have experienced a 'being of total love' who welcomes them, and they believe this to be Jesus or God or some heavenly being. This is reported by Christians, those of other religions, and even those who do not profess to be religious. So I believe the elaborate schemes foisted off on us by some religious denominations — of the rapture of the saved and the damnation of the lost, of the anti-Chirst and the battle of Armageddon — are all a misconception that Jesus will return to subdue an evil world, and we will all be a part of a great social event (at least all who are alive at that time). Nowhere else but in apocalyptic writings is God or Jesus presented as wanting to rule the world as a king or physical leader. The salvation of each individual soul is to recognize the Kingdom of God which has already arrived and is here and now; Revelation was written by St. John on Patmos Island to warn the Christians of his day to persevere, not to prophesy events that are happening in our world today."

Gene Hazlett stopped the tape and looked at Kit, waiting for a reacton. Kit, for his part, was so stunned by these ideas of John Stanton that he couldn't find appropriate words.

"Well, Reverend, just what do you think of that?"

Kit would rather have avoided confrontation at this point and retire to his study to ponder these words he had heard, but he knew some reaction was expected of him, and in his role as minister some reaction was justified.

"That certainly is an interesting theory, isn't it?" was about as much as he could come up with.

"Interesting theory!" Gene fumed. "That is about as sacrilegious as you can get — flying in the face of all we have been taught, from Sunday School on up, it is contrary to the Bible, which is the final word of God, and I think it is time we good church-going people rise up and take a stand for God and the Bible!"

Kit chose his words carefully to avoid adding to Gene's defensiveness. "I will say one thing about Professor Stanton's sermon — it stimulated you to think and moved you to take action, and these are admirable Christian qualities in my opinion."

"Well, I intend to take action, all right, and I believe you should, too. A little damage control is needed, and I hope you preach a few sermons to counteract the misrepresentations he made to this congregation."

Kit assured him this would be done. So the matter rested for several weeks, during which many of those who were most upset about Professor Stanton's sermon had time to get on with their lives. Most of the criticism died down.

16

More Dreams

KIT'S NEXT ENCOUNTER with Messenger came after a particularly trying week in which Duane Taylor refused to attend church because he felt he had been rejected, the Bible study class had broken up in angry accusations over the inerrancy of God's word, and Jean was so disillusioned with some church members that she found it to be a heavy burden just to remain civil to a few of them. Kit tried to relax and get a good night's sleep but was caught in a sort of purgatory between wakefulness and sound slumber where he found himself continually waking to the realization that some insoluble problem was tormenting his mind. Just as he was about to give up all efforts to get to sleep and instead indulge in some midnight reading, he was aware again of the presence of Messenger, who was beckoning to him.

"Come, let me show you the way," Messenger said in a soothing voice. "I have been sent to make an assessment as to whether those of you who call yourselves Christian are growing in the spirit or are falling behind."

"Oh, Messenger, tell me where I've gone wrong and why I can't seem to lead my congregation to follow God's word," pleaded Kit.

"Peace, my son. God is speaking through you to show others the way, but the way is hard and many fall by the wayside.

When your people grow, God rejoices at his creation and when you fail, God mourns. Each of you have an umbilical cord to the creator, and you are fed according to your willingness to accept his sustenance."

"But, try as I may to do Jesus' teaching, I feel I am failing to connect with my church members," cried Kit. "Tell me what I am doing wrong."

"Yours is a noble struggle, my son, and you should not blame yourself. The church is failing in its mission because its members forget that they are the heirs of the disciples of Jesus. The tribe mentality is the continual enemy of the love and grace of Christ, and the churches which the early disciples founded have become institutions of men rather than temples to God."

"But how can I get through to them before it's too late?"

"You can only urge them to be proactive rather than reactive. Help them to see that they are co-creators with God and that the process never ends; they cannot rest on their laurels because evil is always competing for their attention."

"But how do I convince them they are co-creators with God, as you say?" asked Kit.

"You must show them that only as they sense the Holy Spirit within them and then act in a loving way toward their fellow man can the will of God be done in the world. God brought about the first creation, but God expects Christian men and women to join him in creating a better world. You must admonish your congregation against being 'culture Christians' who merely accept the mantle of Christianity bequeathed to them by the culture of the time; they must go beyond mere acquiescence in what their fathers and mothers pass on to them — they must think for themselves and re-examine the roots of their faith."

"But my efforts to develop them spiritually only result in alienating them, and I face rejection for my efforts," said Kit.

"Do not despair, you are more effective than you realize," said Messenger. "You and others like you are on the cutting edge of a great reawakening of the spirit in God's world. You have learned the most important lesson you can learn in this life."

"And what is that?" inquired Kit.

"You have learned that your life is guided by invisible forces and when you cooperate with those forces, no power on earth can stand against you. What may seem to be adversity or rejection by society can be a dawning of a greater consciousness and an invitation to commune with God. St. Paul said, 'We see now as through a glass darkly, but then we shall see him face to face.' This life is a training ground in which you are challenged to seek the unknowable and to experience the mysteries of creation. It is only as you listen to your dreams, interpret your images, and have faith that God is speaking to you that you achieve your full potential. There are so many who have led wasted lives because they would not pause to wonder at the glories of creation. There are so many lives that are uneventful and uninspired because they believe that this is all there is and do not seek a greater dimension to life. You are put here for a purpose, and God's purpose is not to conduct a grand experiment to see whether mankind will survive or be destroyed but to offer eternal oneness with God and to draw out the best in you as a gift to God. Jesus brought the message that living by the rules of conduct is not enough. He taught that your potential for good is unlimited if you only have faith in God's miracles and act on that faith.

"If you will look around you," said Messenger, "you will find this reawakening of the spirit in the lives and attitudes of many faithful Christians. The way may seem difficult, but the rewards of laboring in God's vineyard are great. Do not lose faith."

These words kept reverberating in Kit's mind as he slowly

regained consciousness. "Do not lose faith — do not lose faith — do not lose faith." Kit now saw that his course was clear; no longer would he vacillate between trying to please his congregation and trying to bring them the word of God as he saw it. Messenger had given him the assurance he was seeking — he was on the right course regardless of whether his church would continue to accept him as their pastor.

17

Blowing Our Minds

BY THE TIME the next Sunday arrived, Kit could barely wait to get past the preliminaries and the hymns to the message he had for the congregation of Galilee Methodist Church.

"I am sure that each of you at one time or another has used the expression — that 'blows my mind.' We come up against a phenomenon that our brains are not equipped to decipher, and we simply admit that this set of facts or that set of facts blows our minds! We are told by authors Brand and Yancey in their book *Fearfully and Wonderfully Made* that the DNA in each of our body's cells would fit into an ice cube; yet if the DNA were unwound and joined together end to end, the strand could stretch from the earth to the sun and back more then four hundred times. Also, from the book *Kything the Art of Spiritual Presence* by Savary and Berne, we are told that 95 percent of the ten octillion atoms in our bodies are replaced annually. Some body parts such as bone tissue are eroded and re-formed quickly, while the brain's connective cells are more resistant to being replaced. But after five years you are totally repackaged chemically, renewed down to the very last atom.

"Or, simply take the matter of distances in space. Light travels at 186,000 miles per second, and a light year is the distance that light, traveling at that speed, covers in a year — about six trillion miles. And yet, the constellation Hydra is calculated to be 1.5 billion light years away from us. The universe is so large that light years are not even adequate to measure distances, so scientists have come up with a term — parsecs, which is 3.26 light years — as a means of measuring the great distances in space. And if you really want to hear something that is mind-boggling, let me tell you that scientists' best guess is that the edge of the observable universe is twelve to fifteen billion light years away! And so the faint light we can see in our telescopes from the edge of the observable universe has been traveling for fifteen billion light years just to reach us! And even more hard to believe, if the universe is expanding because of the 'big bang,' there is a point at which the velocity of its expansion approaches the speed of light, and if the rate of expansion equaled the speed of light, then light from those galaxies would never reach us! We would never see them; we would not know they were there!

"Why am I trying to blow your minds today, especially from a church pulpit? Simply this — much of what we know about Jesus is in this same mind-boggling realm. The gospel writers tell us that Jesus could merely touch people and heal them of diseases or deformities. Many times he did not even have to touch them. He could call people back from the dead, and he could cast out demons; we read this and say to ourselves, 'I can't believe he could really do those things. It blows my mind.' Well, that's exactly right. Our minds are not able to understand what God can do. We become unsure of ourselves and frightened when our programmed mind-sets are challenged. We say, 'Jesus couldn't heal people that way — anybody who is modern knows that you heal people with antibiotics and steroids and lazar rays!' Ah, but, my friends, those are only rather recent tools that scientists have discovered; yet people were being healed for thousands of years before those things were developed. You see, the process of healing is something we still don't begin to understand. We have years of medical research behind us, and we have learned about the genes and the enzymes and the DNA, but we still don't understand how the body heals itself or why. We can plant a seed smaller than the end of your little finger, and in a span of years we will have a mighty redwood tree hundreds of feet high and thirty feet around its trunk, but we don't know why it grows or how it grows. It boggles our minds.

"So, it always bothers me when people downplay miracles because they 'go against the laws of nature.' And who, pray tell, are we to be proclaiming what the 'laws of nature' are? We don't begin to understand them after centuries of so-called technological progress; yet I hear well-meaning and properly saved Christians argue that it couldn't have been a miracle that saved Eddie Rickenbacker when he was adrift on the sea and praying for help. They say these things couldn't be a miracle because God does not change his natural laws for us! How do we dare presume to know what God's natural laws are? And how do you tell someone who is healed from cancer that God won't change his natural laws for us when we pray to him! When the disciples marveled at Jesus' miracles, he said to them: 'Even greater things than these you will do in my name.'

"Jesus said to us that whenever two or more of us are gathered together in prayer, there he will be in the midst of us and that whatsoever we ask of him, if we believe in him we will receive it. But do we believe this? Have we ever really tried out this source of great power? Can we bring ourselves to experience a different level of consciousness, or are we just going to stay in our same old rut, having been programmed for years to believe that science is our God? Will we continue to believe only in the power of science?

"Today we stand on the threshold of a new awakening to spirituality. We acknowledge that it may blow our minds. We cannot understand it. But there is a great hunger for spiritual sustenance. There is a new willingness to believe in things we cannot prove. Even scientists are admitting that there is so much that we do not know and that some things happen for reasons that we cannot rationally explain. People are meeting in small groups all over this land—interdenominationally or non-denominationally — to seek a spiritual experience. People are meeting to pray for physical and mental healing. People are meeting to pray for peace."

Kit paused to survey his congregation. There was not a sound in the sanctuary. All eyes were on him and all attention was riveted on him. And it was 12:55.

"I challenge you today to see your potential — your heritage — yes, your charge: To revitalize the Christian religion as a force that can again sweep the world as it did in the second and third centuries and that can indeed bring the Kingdom of God into every human life."

Kit later couldn't remember just what happened after he finished the sermon. There were the usual closing hymns and a benediction and the usual greetings at the door of the church, but it seemed there was more than the usual earnestness in the handshakes at the door, more than the usual silent hugs and meaningful looks and speechless expressions of support and affirmation. Not one parishioner paused to say they "enjoyed" the sermon. No one complained about their physical condition or mentioned politics. It was a different congregation that left the church that day, but Kit couldn't help wondering if it would bring about real change in the outlook of the congregation of Galilee Methodist Church.

18

Angels

KIT WAS AWARE that Jean had been having a number of treatments by Duane Taylor and that her arthritis was showing marked improvement as a result. What he was not prepared for was Jean's announcement to him that in addition to her images, which Jean was still experiencing whenever she was meditating, she was encountering something different at these healing sessions — she was actually seeing angels.

"I know you're going to think I am losing my mind," Jean announced one day, "but I am really becoming conscious of the presence of angels, and it is happening every time I have a healing session with Duane Taylor. At first I was aware of people in the room and I would mention it to Duane, but he couldn't see them. He never ridiculed me; as a matter of fact, he could feel them empowering him, but only recently has he begun to be aware of them as I am."

"And what are these angels like?" asked Kit.

"They come in all sizes and wear different colored robes. Some are all in white and appear to be delighted to be there and are assisting Duane in some way in doing the healing. Others are very large and solemn and have blue or brown robes. I think they all have wings, and since I see them face to face I only see the tips of their wings over their shoulders. Also, some are small, like children, and I was aware of them when I went into the empty church sanctuary the other day to pray. They were flying around up near the ceiling of the sanctuary and singing and seemed quite joyful."

"Is there any particular occasion that causes you to experience them, or are they there all the time?" asked Kit.

"Oh, I am sure they are there all the time," said Jean, "but I only experience them when I am meditating or being treated by Duane. You do believe me, don't you?"

"Jean, I have the greatest confidence in you, and even though my rational mind might tend to dismiss them as hallucinations, my spiritual self tells me you are experiencing a different level of consciousness that not many people feel, and the answer is — yes, I believe you."

"Well, it is very disturbing that I can't feel comfortable telling anyone other than you and Duane Taylor and Debbie Miller about them. I am afraid if the congregation ever got word that your wife was seeing angels, we would both be ridden out of town on a rail."

"Do the angels ever say anything to you, and what do you think they are trying to accomplish?" asked Kit.

"Oh yes, they give me messages and tell me what they are doing, and it always has to do with helping me or helping someone else. They seem to be guiding Duane in knowing just where in my body is the pain that needs relieving, and they always seem to be so eager to help and so pleased that someone acknowledges their presence."

"I think it is interesting that angels play such a prominent part in both the Old and New Testaments; yet, we had almost written them off until recently. There seems to be renewed interest in them," said Kit. "After all, angels appeared to Abram and Sari before they became Abraham and Sarah, and they announced that Sarah would bear a child to Abraham. Angels rescued Lot from Sodom and Gomorrah, Jacob wrestled all night with an angel, and the story of the birth of Jesus is filled with accounts of the announcement of his coming and the directions to the Holy Family to escape to Egypt and then when to return. You would think that the most important aspect of the Christian religion would be an unqualified acceptance of the presence of angels in our lives, and yet modern-day religion either dismisses them as delusions of the mind or as evil spirits associated with Satan. How could I get across to our congregation that people really do experience angels even today?"

"I don't know whether you can, but please don't mention my experience with angels to anyone in our church. I don't think they are ready to hear it," replied Jean.

"That's just it — I keep running into this all the time. If they aren't ready to hear it, then why aren't they? And how does one preacher in one small town get through to them that there may be a lot they are missing out on because they can't abandon old habits or embrace a new level of consciousness?"

"I guess the best you can do is keep exposing them to fresh ideas; if they won't listen, at least you should not blame yourself."

Kit found himself preparing for next Sunday's sermon with a new resolve to reach the most resistant of his constituents and to find some way to introduce them to God's love.

19

A Time of Testing

KIT SPENT MORE than the usual amount of time preparing for the next Sunday's sermon. He was not unmindful of Giles Graham's coolness towards him or of Gene Hazlett's admonition to respond to John Stanton's sermon, nor of Fred Findlay's rebellion at having Duane Taylor as a new member. But the latest reassuring words from Messenger kept echoing through his mind as he settled himself in his study to plan a message that hopefully would bring some insight to the congregation. The words came easily to his mind and he couldn't help but feel that a hand was guiding him as he began composing the sermon.

"This morning I want to bring you a message. This message is very real, but if I told you I received it from a messenger in a dream or a vision, would it mean any less to you? I have hesitated to preach this sermon because I know it departs from what you are accustomed to, but the message is important and it is urgent. There may not be much time, so I feel it important that we be aware of what is happening. And what is happening is that we are losing the very essence of the Christian movement. We have wandered so far from the inspiration of the apostles that we have lost all inspiration. We no longer believe in miracles or in visions or in angels. And yet the original Christian movement was entirely caught up with miracles and visions and dreams and angels. We experience someone in our community who can heal our afflictions as Jesus did, but rather than follow him as the early disciples did, we reject him and refuse him membership in our church. We believe the worst about him and rather than expressing love and acceptance, we spread idle rumors about him. We turn a cold ear to the message of our Savior that we should love our enemies and do good to them who despitefully use us because society says we must destroy those whom society has crippled. 'A life for a life,' we say, and we try to justify this through the words of the Old Testament. The early church recognized the futility of the Jewish laws of retribution; the disciples knew that by doing good to those who harm you, you are heaping coals of fire on their heads.

"We have so imbedded in our being the learned behavior of centuries of church doctrine that we have conveniently forgotten to think for ourselves and thus have lost the freshness and vitality of the words of Jesus that the disciples knew. We will accept God's word from the Bible only if it comes couched in the stilted, convenient phrases we have learned by rote, without a thought as to whether such words were placed in that great book only because committees of bishops and presbyters prescribed what we should believe and rejected as apocryphal all other writings about Jesus.

"The time of our trial and testing is near at hand but not the end of the world by an authoritarian God shedding great disasters on us to punish us, as many would believe, but because of our own failure to recognize the great love of God extended to each of us but which we reject out of hand as being too simple a solution for the world. If our society is disintegrating, it is not because of what was written in the Book of Revelation but because we still haven't learned to accept God's grace extended to us as it was in the Garden of Eden. The lesson is there, written by a very wise and insightful author in the book of Genesis, and we still haven't got the point. We think the whole message is to resist evil, and if we can't resist then we must repent of our wrongdoing; whereas the message is clear — God who created you is continually reaching out to you. Yet you are reluctant to respond in the only way you can respond — by loving God in return. The problems of the world can be solved in just that simple process of returning the love of God, yet we try every other way in hopes of avoiding Armageddon.

"We say we expect the Kingdom of God to come in our day. Some expect this to come with great fanfare and a cataclysmic world event; yet Jesus, the son of God, came to tell us that the Kingdom of God is 'within' us. This has many implications for the Christian. This seemingly unreachable goal of achieving the Kingdom of God is within reach of each one of us; it is not a status to be achieved nor a reward to be received. It is already here, and each of us needs only to recognize it. It is not out there among society but is within the private consciousness of each of us. Each person, no matter how lowly or exalted, no matter how humble or powerful, no matter where he or she is on the social scale, has an equal right to share in the Kingdom, but this means acknowledging that there is a higher level of consciousness than the one we normally operate in, a level not confined to time or space, a level we cannot quantify or reach through our senses, a level we cannot ever describe or achieve through our intellect. It is a state of being that can only be achieved by giving oneself over completely to the love of God and putting all else in second place, and if the individual Christian would do this, many of the problems faced by churches today would fall away.

"It is not that we are called upon to abandon the church, but it is that the church has abandoned the nurturing of the presence of the Holy Spirit in our lives, and this must be restored in some way. If each Christian institution in the land placed first and foremost in its program a way to encourage its members to commune with God — if every person who calls himself or herself Christian would figuratively extend their antennas to seek to receive a message from the creator — perhaps we could begin to return to the climate in which the early church prospered.

"Jesus conversed with two disciples on the road to Emmaus, but they were so caught up in the traumatic events of the crucifixion that they couldn't recognize who was trying to communicate with them. It was only when they shared intimate moments with him in meditation and prayer that they became aware of who this stranger was. This is the way it must always be. The Christian religious movement cannot remake society by conforming to society and then trying to convert it by precept and example. The recognition of God's message must come to each individual through a willingness to listen and learn, through inspiration, and the acceptance of the unqualified love of God offered to each person willing to receive it. God did not choose to threaten his earthly children with punishment and great disasters (except in some beliefs going back to Old Testament times). God chose to give society a chance to redeem itself and to come to recognize him as creator by subtle, incremental steps over centuries of time. Jesus came not as a temporal ruler who would impose a Christian code upon subject peoples, but as a member of the common people, undistinguished by power or position, who caused his disciples to think as he slowly and painstakingly planted God's message in their minds.

"Surely the creator of the universe and all that's in it could have come in power and cast out all the sinners and rewarded the faithful; thus, God's kingdom could have been assured on earth. But the creator did not choose to bring the kingdom in this manner. The kingdom was to exist in each individual who was willing to accept God's love and listen for God's wisdom. And down through the ages, society has slowly been changed by this process of transformation from within each individual. I do not believe that God plans to transform society by one final act of rapture of the faithful and destruction of the wicked. This does not fit with God's way of dealing with his creation in the past. It does not fit with Jesus' words that the kingdom is not of this world, but is within each of us."

Kit paused and suddenly noticed that the hour was much later than he had realized. He had been composing this sermon without the trial and error and periods of anguish which usually accompanied the genesis of a sermon. He also felt a strange warmth in his study and the distinct impression that someone else was in the room. Without thinking, he turned to view the monitor on his computer once again and read there words that he could not remember composing: "The kingdom of God is within you. It is here and now."

20

The Trial

THE DEFINING MOMENT for the Galilee Methodist Church arrived with the meeting of the staff- parish committee. Kit had known for some time that a movement was afoot to recommend to the district superintendent that he not be returned as pastor of the church. This saddened Kit, but it did not create in him a state of shock as it might have if he had felt that all was going smoothly and he was being rejected because he was not properly ministering to his congregation. Kit felt justified in all of his efforts to bring his flock to an encounter with God. The words of Messenger kept going through his mind, "Do not lose faith." Kit couldn't help but recall the words of St. Paul from Second Timothy, "I am being poured out as a libation and the time of my departure has come. I have fought the good fight, I have finished the race, I have kept the faith."

These words strengthened him as he appeared before the staff-parish committee to take up the question of evaluation of the pastor.

"Kit, you are aware that there have been some complaints about your ministry here," began Chairman Fred Findlay. "The purpose of calling this meeting of the committee is to air any complaints and do the evaluation of you that the discipline requires and report our evaluation to the district superintendent. Also, it is to give you a due process hearing so you may

respond to any such complaints. Let me say at the beginning that we are not here to judge you. We all respect you, and we are aware that you have brought us some new ideas. As a matter of fact, it is some of these new ideas that have caused some of the congregation to make complaints to us. We plan to read you the complaints, and then there are quite a few of the congregation who have asked to say something in
your behalf. As we have time we have agreed to bring in those members to have their say. As you know, we are required by the church discipline to evaluate you annually and if this committee feels your assignment here is not a good fit, we'll recommend to the district superintendent that you be moved."

At this point Fred paused and looked at Kit as if he expected a reply, but Kit only nodded.

Fred continued, "Now, does anyone on the committee have anything to say?"

There was a long, awkward pause while Fred waited, looking at each member in turn, but the members averted their eyes, looking down at their evaluation sheets or shuffling them. Bessie Wilson was suddenly overcome by an uncontrolled fit of coughing and had to leave the room. Giles Graham couldn't seem to find a paper he was looking for.

"Well," said Fred, "who will start this off? I know I have heard each of you make comments about things we should bring up to the pastor, so here is your chance."

"I will start it off," volunteered Giles Graham. "You all know that my daughter left this church because she felt there wasn't anything here for the youth. It was one of the saddest moments of my life when she left the church she was brought up in. She's now is a member of an ultra-liberal group that, as far as I can tell, doesn't even believe as we do and has all kinds of weird worship services. I understand she talked to you, Reverend, about our youth program before she left, and it was because of your unresponsiveness and unwillingness to change that she and some others from her Sunday School class moved their membership elsewhere."

Kit considered whether his best course would be to endure the committee's criticisms in silence, as Jesus had done before the Sanhedrin, or to defend himself as both Peter and Paul had done. He decided that if he kept silent a wrong impression would be left with the committee about the true nature of his encounter with Giles' daughter Shirley.

"As a matter of fact, it was the Free Spirit Sunday School class that was involved, Giles, and your daughter's request was to abandon the time-honored Sunday school material provided by the conference, which Methodist churches have used for generations, and to study, instead, a modern book written about an atheist who receives a revelation that is reported as a message from God. When she asked permission to have the class use this as study material, I tried to bring this request to the administrative board, but since she wanted an answer immediately and the board didn't meet for another three weeks, I told her I thought some of our standard Sunday school material would be more appropriate. She left and has never been back to our church as far as I know."

This information seemed to stun Giles Graham. Since he didn't respond, Kit continued, "I have since come to the conclusion that I should have spent more time trying to structure a program that would keep intelligent, inquisitive young people in our church and would meet their needs as they seek inspiration. It is well known that youth will ask questions and will seek a spiritual experience; if we don't respond properly to their quest, we will lose them either to a faith that will meet their needs or, in many cases, we may lose them to the hippie communes and the drug culture. I only regret that I didn't have the courage to at least meet Shirley halfway and give her some challenging ideas — perhaps even lead a discussion on the book she wanted to study — and she and her friends would still be active members and future leaders of our church. So, yes, I admit that in this I failed."

Fred Findlay cleared his throat and moved to another subject. Since Bessie Wilson had returned to the room during this discussion, Fred turned to her and asked her to repeat a complaint she had made to him recently.

"Oh, well, I don't really have any criticism of Rev. Benson," Bessie haltingly replied. "It's just that for years I could come to this church and feel that my life was secure and all was well with the world. As long as we got a good message of the love of God, I felt my personal problems were overcome, and I felt completely comfortable. I could sit in the sanctuary after a good sermon and a few of the old familiar hymns and feel that all life's struggles were worth it just because my religion would save me from the evils I could see all around me in the world. I just don't come to church to be preached to about my responsibilities to God; I come to find solace and peace. Yet lately whenever I leave church on Sunday morning, I leave so upset that I can't even enjoy eating out after church."

Fred Findlay looked at Kit expecting some response.

"The only thing I can say in answer is that I guess I have a different philosophy about what Christianity should be about. When I consider what the first Christians had to endure in order to remain in the faith, I can't understand why anyone would expect to be made comfortable when they come to church. If it is comfort and self-satisfaction we are looking for, there are other agencies we can turn to, but I believe that Christians must be continually challenged and must continually grow in their faith. We never get to a point where we can sit back and smugly say, 'I am saved, so I need no longer make any effort to seek God's word.' As a matter of fact, the Bible teaches us that we learn through our mistakes and our trials and tribulations and that many times the way we find God is when the going is tough. I would feel it was a betrayal of my ministerial oath if I only tried to please and flatter the congregation and did not challenge them."

At this, Bessie Wilson looked properly chastised and did not wish to say any more, so Fred Findlay began on his evaluation.

"Kit, you know from past conversations that we have had our disagreements. I cannot accept that we should love murderers or that the second coming of Christ is just a story-tale, but I believe my most serious criticism of your ministry here is that it has allowed such things as the charlatan faith healer to continue his operation. Instead of rejecting him because of the rumors about him and your wife, you invite him into the congregation. How do you explain that?"

"Well, Fred, first of all I don't believe as Christians we should accept idle rumors. I believe we owe it to our fellow Christians to give them the benefit of a doubt and to try to rely on true facts and even then, if we don't like the facts, to try to be as charitable as Jesus was. You remember he told the mob that was preparing to stone the woman taken in adultery, 'Let him who is without sin cast the first stone'; we, as his followers, can do no less. I am convinced that Duane Taylor is a deeply spiritual Christian, and his success rate at personal healings can only be because of his deep faith. Simply because he professes to heal in the same way Jesus and his disciples did, rather than the way we've been taught throughout the centuries is the *only* way to heal the body doesn't mean we should reject him. As a matter of fact, if we were truly spiritual beings seeking God's grace, we would be trying to copy his methods. Think what a great revivial of faith would occur if many members of this church were to be able to heal others as Duane Taylor does. It could be happening, and the only reason it isn't happening is because we do not have the faith to make it happen."

There was silence in the room for a moment until one of the invited church members who was not on the committee began to clap her hands. Suddenly other members began to applaud, and Fred had to rap his knuckles on the table trying to restore order. "Let the committee come to order. We allowed you members into the committee hearings in order to hear what you have to say, but let's not have public displays of emotion here. We are engaged in our charge to evaluate the minister; this is not a popularity contest."

"Next we will hear from Gene Hazlett about a complaint he has," said Fred.

"Yes, well, I really don't have much to say about our pastor. I, for one, believe his sermons have a lot to say to us. I guess my criticism is that he invited a layman to give a sermon which was almost blasphemous, in my opinion. Of course, Kit was not directly responsible and didn't, I believe, know ahead of time what Stanton was going to say, but I personally played the tape for you, Kit, after your vacation and you promised to respond to Stanton's ideas about the second coming in a sermon. I don't recall that you ever did that."

"What can I say?" responded Kit. "I was as surprised to hear John's interpretation as you were, but I certainly can't consider it blasphemous just because he sees the second coming as a personal experience and not as a global event. I think this is exactly the kind of situation where God intended us to use these ingenious minds of ours to reason out our own conclusions and not to take some doctrine or tradition that has been handed down to use as the inevitable outcome of things. I respect Professor Stanton for his well-reasoned conclusions. Who are we to say that he is wrong, much less blasphemous?"

"And what did seminary teach you about dreams and visions and angels?" asked Fred Findlay. "I wasn't aware that was standard study material for ministers, and yet your sermons, moving and thought-provoking as they may be, have indicated that some of them are based upon your personal dreams, and you have implied that angels affect our daily lives. I don't hear other pastors telling these things to their congregations."

"It's true, I did not learn these things in seminary," responded Kit. "Our training programs for the ministry seem to be patterned for a very general background in the Christian faith and to appeal to the lowest common denominator. We are given historical material about our faith but little about inspiration. I believe that if a minister is to properly serve his congregation, he or she must be inspired by the Holy Spirit and that this is what ministry is all about. Jesus promised us at Pentecost that although he would depart physically from our world as all human beings do, as a divine representative he would send us a presence to be with us and care for our spiritual needs. So he sent the Holy Spirit to us. But somewhere along the way in the history of our religion, this has been de-emphasized and disregarded so that the true relationship of Jesus to his disciples has been distorted from what existed in the original churches. I make no apologies for going back to those things that made the first churches vital — dreams, visions, angels and physical healings. Every pastor should, in my opinion, emphasize the importance of these things. Just because our training schools have chosen to disregard them does not mean we shouldn't incorporate them into our worship services."

Fred Findlay again looked at each of his committee members as if to inquire whether there weren't more subjects that hadn't been covered. "Carl Hawes, you had a criticism of our pastor. Would you like to express it now?"

"Oh, I don't know that it is directed particularly at Kit. My concern is the modern tendency to attack the Bible, attack the organized church, and as a result our society is falling apart. We have drugs, pre-marital sex, murders in our streets, and I can't help but think that if we went back to the strict religious codes of our grandfather's day, we wouldn't tolerate all this evil going on in our society. Some of us were brought up to believe that the Bible is the word of God and what the minister tells us on Sunday is to be our guide during the week. We know that to do wrong is to sin. We used to use the word sin in a meaningful way. You heard it from the pulpit, and religious folk were not afraid to point out what was sinful in our daily lives. Today there seems to be this great permissiveness about everything we do. The Jesus freaks use Jesus' name but bomb out on drugs, and the high school senior class sees nothing wrong with going to motels all night on graduation day. Committees of distinguished theologians get together to pooh-pooh the gospels and try to prove that Jesus not only was not resurrected, but even that he wasn't really crucified. Our young people seek after New Age gurus. The world is going to the dogs in a hand basket."

Carl Hawes paused, somewhat embarrassed at the extent that he had been carried away, but since no one volunteered to respond, he continued more quietly, "I guess what I am trying to tell our pastor is that I believe he should be preaching on how the church can fight back against sin in all its forms and how we need to get back to the Bible and respect the doctrines of the church and put down dissent wherever we find it. I don't find that you, Kit, have done that. I believe you are too easygoing on those ideas that would lead our faithful astray and that you haven't honored the traditions of the church."

Kit thought for a moment before answering, "It is hard to know how to respond to the wide array of charges you have made. You have put on my shoulders the responsibility for right-ing all of the wrongs of our society in a day when our religion has come to conform to our culture instead of being the yeast that requires our culture to conform to our religion. You say we should go back to the traditions of the church, and yet I have spent most of my ministry trying to explain to those who would listen that our church's traditions, built up over the ages since Jesus sent the Holy Spirit to energize us, have been watered down and in some cases changed completely from the early Christian faith. Our traditions show us a church that early in its history seized temporal power from kings and ruled its members with an iron hand, putting many faithful souls to death. The witch trials are a part of our 'traditions' — the senseless murdering of young females because the church hierarchy believed they were instruments of Satan, simply because they heard a call from God to try to correct the evils in their society.

"The Christian religion had not survived one hundred years before the equal participation of all sexes in worship services was ruthlessly stamped out by early bishops and presbyters who found that they could exercise great power over the lives of their congregations, and they jealously guarded that power. Jesus himself was outspoken in his criticism of the religious leaders of the Jews in his day, saying, 'Woe unto you, scribes and pharisees, for you are like whited sepulchures which appear beautiful on the outside, but within are full of dead bones and uncleanness.' Jesus did not have a lot to say about the social ills of homosexuality, infidelity or drunkeness, but his attacks on the religious leaders of his day were scathing. Should we be afraid to point out the same type of hypocrisy in the church today?

"In Jesus' day the Jewish religion had such rigid rules that acts of love and compassion to one's fellow man were overshadowed by the need to make a good show of one's faithfulness to the 'tradition.' The Pharisees told the Jews what was best for their salvation and that was that. Today we have religious denominations that operate out of rigid traditions and overlook Jesus' precepts of love and compassion. We have TV preachers and leaders of conservative denominations that tell us we are sure to go to hell if we don't believe as they do. I have simply felt it my duty to go back to what Jesus taught the first disciples and then to overlook or disregard the historical influences on our church as being irrelevant to the truth of the gospels."

At this point, Liddy Harshman, head of the education and outreach committee, asked to be heard. "I want to speak in behalf of Rev. Benson," she began. "I was raised in a very conservative church, and I know I have trouble departing from the traditional thinking about the role of the church and Christian education, but I want to give Kit credit for exposing us to some new ideas that I believe are valid and yet hard for some of us to accept. I have seen us gain some new members, not because of fear that they would go to hell if they didn't join the church, but because they were seeking something that other churches didn't give them. If Kit is to be faulted because we lost some of the Free Spirit Sunday School class, then we need to have material available to satisfy inquiring minds and not just to restate the church's position on social issues. I think he has done a good job; we need more Kit Bensons in our society."

With this, some of those present applauded again, and again Chairman Findlay had to rap for order. There followed endorsements by John Stanton, Edith Frazier and others until, due to the lateness of the hour, Fred Findlay announced that the committee would meet again the next week to go into executive session to discuss what the evaluation would be.

21

The Kingdom of God

A FEELING OF IMPENDING DOOM permeated the Galilee church in the two weeks following the meeting of the staff-parish committee. Some of Kit's faithful supporters in the congregation urged him to answer the complaints of the committee in a fiery sermon that would put them in their place. Some even suggested starting a new church and asking Kit to lead it. But Kit recognized that to do so would not solve any problems and even to discuss it would further polarize the congregation. Kit felt that the problem was not one of attempting to satisfy the traditionalist and conservative members of the church but to keep getting God's message through to those in the church who would accept it. What would happen to this church if he were transferred? Kit could see the Fred Findlays and the Gene Hazletts leading the less strong-willed members back to the comfortable, traditional, "don't rock the boat" condition that prevented the church body from coming alive with spiritual growth. They would be perfectly happy with a low-key pastor who would spoon-feed them the time-honored do's and don'ts of the institutional church, and they would never be challenged to think through their religious beliefs or to seek inspirational ideas.

Kit confided to Jean that he had a feeling that the staff-parish committee would contact the district superintendent to try to replace him as pastor.

"It's enough to cause a person to lose all the Christian faith one ever had the way a few people in the congregation can be so blind to what is happening. Don't they want to be closer to God, or are they content just to attend church suppers and give to missions and imagine their lives are ideal examples of Christian piety?" mused Jean over the dinner table. "Why don't you just resign and see if you can find a congregation that is more open-minded?"

"That would abandon those who will listen to those who won't and would be a poor example of a spiritual leader. Besides, Messenger keeps encouraging me that I am doing the right thing and that a continual emphasis on the spiritual is what is needed to reawaken society to the true message of the Christian religion. I cannot let Messenger down."

Within the week, word came that Duane Taylor had been charged by the State Board of Healing Arts with practicing medicine without a license and so had moved out of the community and out of Kit's and Jean's life.

"I never dreamed that being a pastor would be so hard," cried Jean. "Don't these people know they are crucifying you just as surely as our Lord was crucified so long ago? Don't they appreciate the struggle we had to get through seminary and then trying to live on an associate minister's salary, and now to be treated like this ..."

Jean's words trailed off into sobs of anguish while Kit tried to find words that would heal her pain. All that would come to mind were the words of Jesus on the cross, "Father, forgive them, for they know not what they do."

Kit longed for another visit with Messenger but had been sleeping fitfully and no dream seemed to come to him bringing any message of relief. He knew he must prepare a sermon for the next Sunday no matter what the staff-parish committee might decide, so he developed an idea suggested to him earlier by Jean after the sermon he gave some months ago about being born again. As he sat at his word processor the words began to appear on the monitor.

"A few months ago, I spoke to you about Nicodemus coming to Jesus to ask him about the kingdom of God. You will recall that Nicodemus, the good Pharisee, already thought he had salvation but was told by Jesus, 'You must be born from above.' Some of you have since asked me how this is to be done. It is all well and good for Jesus to say, 'You must be born again', or 'You must be born from above,' but how does one go about doing this? I think the answer is found in Luke 17:21, where Jesus tells his disciples 'The kingdom of God is within you.' Scholars have differed over the correct translation of the preposition from the Greek. The normal use of the Greek word is 'within' — the kingdom of God is within you. And this is the wording used in the King James version. But the Revised Standard Version translates the preposition to mean 'in the midst of you' or 'among you.' You can see that it makes a great deal of difference which translation is used. On the one hand, if the kingdom is 'within us,' Jesus was saying that God exists in each one of us and that the kingdom is a new state of being where we recognize his presence. If the kingdom of God is 'in the midst of us' or 'among us,' then apparently he is talking about his personal presence bringing a new philosophy, which will influence a new social order. Just which is the correct meaning of the preposition we cannot know for sure, but a book entitled *Fearfully and Wonderfully Made* by Dr. Paul Brand and Phillip Yancey proposes the idea that, indeed, God is within each of us. Dr. Brand, a noted hand surgeon who researched the treatment of leprosy for eighteen years in India, states:

We carry within us not just the image of, or the philosophy of, or faith in, but the actual substance of God. One staggering consequence credits us with the spiritual genes of Christ: as we stand before God, we are judged on the basis of Christ's perfection, not our unworthiness. 'If anyone is in Christ, he is a new creation; the old has gone, the new has come! God made him who had no sin to be sin for us, so that in him we might become the righteousness of God. (2nd. Cor. 5:17, 21)

"Brand compares true Christianity to the human body's DNA. He states that every cell in the body possesses a genetic code so complete that the entire body could be reassembled from information in any one of the body's cells. This, of course, is the basis for the theory of cloning.

"Brand carries this comparison further to say that each of us in the Christian community becomes genetically like Christ himself because we belong to his Body. DNA passes on to the body a specific identity to each new cell. Jesus has infused us with spiritual life that is just as real as natural life. He described the process to Nicodemus in John 3: 1-8 when he said, 'You must be born from above.'

"He also said, 'I am in the Father and you are in me, and I am in you.' He said, 'I am the vine, you are the branches,' and, of course, Paul said, 'Do you not realize that Christ is in you?'

"Brand also says, 'The process of joining Christ's Body may at first seem like a renunciation. I no longer have full independence. Ironically, however, renouncing my old value system — in which I had to compete with other people on the basis of power, wealth, and talent — and committing myself to Christ, the Head, abruptly frees me. My sense of competition fades. No longer do I have to bristle against life, seizing ways to prove myself. In my new identity, my ideal has become to live my life in such a way that people around me recognize Jesus Christ and His love, not my own set of distinctive qualities. My worth and acceptance are enveloped in Him. I have found this process of renunciation and commitment to be healthy, relaxing and wholly good.'

"The author goes on to point out that when we look at the history of the church, we find we have misunderstood or at least have not followed Jesus' teaching about God being in us. Instead we have developed a legalism that says God is out there somewhere, and we must conform to the guidelines to even approach him. This system of legalism is a carry-over from the Jewish Torah, and Jesus was outspoken in condemning it. No other issue — not pornography, adultery, violence, or the other things that most rankle Christians today — inspired more outbursts from Jesus. He criticized the Pharisees, who were pious Jews who devoted their lives to following God. They obeyed each minute law in the Old Testament and sent missionaries to spread the law to others, yet Jesus denounced them, and he did so because far from coming closer to God, legalism actually lowered one's sights. Legalism spells out an exact external code, and if one doesn't meet it, one is rejected. Legalists miss the whole point — that the Christian religion is a free gift from God whether we deserve it or not. And when we accept the gift, then God is within us."

Kit paused and reviewed his handiwork. This should help people answer the question of how they can be born from above as spoken of by Jesus, and it should be something most of his congregation could relate to and accept. He couldn't help but think that Messenger would approve of this approach to the congregation.

When Sunday morning arrived, Kit had polished his sermon and added a closing prayer. He felt a feeling of confidence as he took the pulpit for the morning service.

22

The Final Decision

THE DECISION of the staff-parish committee came after a long and heated session in which tempers flared and charges and counter-charges were exchanged. As dutifully reported by Liddy Harshman, the controversy over Kit's stewardship of the church centered around his defense of Duane Taylor's healing and his acceptance of John Stanton's views on the Second Coming. Some on the committee had taken offense at Kit's attempt to illustrate the pervasiveness of visions and angels in the New Testament by cutting out all such references from a Bible chosen for this purpose, and as a result the charge was that he publicly desecrated God's Holy Word from the pulpit. The failed Bible study class and the disillusionment of the youth also added fuel to the fire. To Fred Findlay fell the duty of informing Kit that the committee would ask the district superintendent to replace him. Fred made the announcement in his usual blunt but hesitating manner.

"We all want you to know, Kit, that there is nothing personal in our decision. You have been here five years and have made many friends, and all of us acknowledge that your stewardship of our church has been, well, dedicated and well-intended. It's just not what a majority of the committee feels is right for our church. Some come on Sunday morning seeking assurance for their lives and seeking refuge from a society that is growing more and more violent; yet we are made to feel uncomfortable about our traditions and uncertain of what is expected of us. We are losing members, and our youth program has all but disappeared. Some important members of our congregation have been offended by the type of person you have tried to bring in to our membership, and we have lost the services of some of our most faithful members at a time when we should be drawing closer together. We don't seem to have any cohesiveness in the congregation anymore," Fred finally paused for breath and looked to Kit to respond.

"And what will you tell the district superintendent that your needs are as a congregation?" inquired Kit.

This seemed to stun Fred, as if needs hadn't been considered, and he was at a loss to respond. "Well," he faltered, "I guess we just need someone who will be there to care for us when crises come along in our lives. We want a good pulpit man who can bring in new members and raise the church's budget and not be always criticizing us for what we do."

"I see," said Kit. "Well, I hope you find what you are wanting."

With this the conversation ended, and the message was sent to the district superintendent to replace Kit with someone who would be a better "fit" for the congregation of Galilee First United Methodist Church.

For Kit, it raised the dilemma of whether to try again with another congregation, to bring them to a spiritual understanding of God's message or whether there were other avenues he could seek to try to break through their complacency and self-sufficiency. Messenger's admonition not to lose faith kept coming back to Kit, as well as Paul's words from Second Timothy, "I have fought the good fight, I have finished the course, I have kept the faith."

23

The Final Sermon

THIS WAS Kit Benson's last Sunday to address his congregation. Some of the members of the congregation felt a sense of sadness, some resignation, some concern, and, of course, for some a feeling of relief that at last someone new would be coming to serve them. But regardless of their feelings about Kit's tenure as pastor, the church was filled to overflowing with members eager to hear what the pastor would say in his parting remarks to his flock. Kit had prepared well and had no hesitation in what he wanted to say.

"This will be my last message to you. I would like to be able to lead you into what I believe is God's true message for his creation, but there are pitfalls on every side. Instead of letting our vision lead us to him, we become distracted with logic and reason. Instead of admitting that there may be a level of consciousness higher and greater than our mere human minds can conceive of, we engage in petty bickering about this dogma or that dogma that some exalted human leader has prescribed to cure human ills. Instead of seeking to kneel in awe before his glory expressed in a great chorale or a gorgeous sunset or a quiet mountain stream, we compete with each other to try to prove that our beliefs are better than someone else's beliefs; we admit only what our limited experience and our prejudiced minds will accept. We do not expand our minds with new experiences or admit that there may be much more that we cannot and are not intended to understand than that which we can comprehend. We waste our precious God-given time on earth trying to deal with life's ambiguities rather than seeking after those things that were both here before we were and that extend beyond our lives. Those of us who see visions and dream dreams are suspected of being irrelevant while those who play at life's games are either rewarded as being successful or cast by the wayside as being of no worth.

"The Bible is a history of centuries of human interaction with God. Throughout history God has been reaching out to us as his creation, and the test has always been: do we respond to that reaching out? Educated Christian scholars call it God's grace, and it has been with us since the beginning of time, but we seldom stop to take the time to give thanks for it. We can engage in endless debate about whether one statement taken from the Holy Scriptures is inconsistent with another taken from another place in the Scripture, we can question whether every word in our King James or our Revised Standard Version of the Bible is the inerrant word of God, or we can see the larger picture of a loving creator who brings us hints of the life he has planned for us hereafter through the fallible written accounts of those disciples and human witnesses who tried to understand what God was saying to them.

"We can shout our creeds at each other until someone succumbs to our will, and then we feel we have led them to salvation. When will we learn that the creator of all things simply wants us to seek him? We were told long ago that he does not want our sacrifices. He does not want us to bargain with him for position, power or material things. He reaches out to us with a simple offer of love, and our only obligation is love in return. We have worshipped a God of vengeance, of retribution, and a God of battle, when all the time he has been seeking to draw us to him though his true nature of healer, comforter and lover. How many centuries have to go by before we learn that the band of inspired disciples at Pentecost represent the best example of the community that God expects us to embrace? Why have we blindly followed those who led us away from the Christian doctrine and into the maze of human error with our Crusades, our Inquisitions, our institutionalized dogma? Why do we still, after all these millennia of Christian teaching and example pursue our man-made gods of wealth, power, status, and self-indulgence? We fret and complain about others in our society who don't conform to our man-made standards of conduct without realizing that standards set by man will not prevail against the ultimate will of God. We treat nature as if it were given us to exploit for our own greed without stopping to realize that God intended us to be good stewards of his creative gifts and not thieves and desecrators of them.

"Each of us views reality only through our own eyes and our own experiences. Each individual experiences his or her own world, and how we view that world depends on the extent to which we have responded to the great God who created it. The saintly individual will see the good things God has done for him or her; the evil person will see only the opportunities of corrupting and exploiting others. It is the same world, the same creation, the same society, but each person moves within it according to the extent they have been visited by God's holy grace. Some are born in societies that provide little opportunity to know God's grace, and it is our responsibility to see that they have that opportunity. Others will not recognize the grace of God when it is available to them and will miss forever their chance of salvation.

"I have been with you as your pastor for five years now, and it is your will that I move on to another parish. I accept this without anger or resentment but only with sadness that I have not been adequate to the task God sent me to perform. In trying to lead our young people to God, I tried to conform them to a prescribed doctrine that church leaders laid down for the education of our youth. I didn't realize that youth are seeking for a meaningful experience with God; they reject hyprocrisy and pretense and seek alternative ways to accept God's summons to them. I failed to see that, and as a result our youth programs have been sterile, and many youth have left our church. I tried to provide meaningful Bible study of a type that is not arbitrary or punitive but leads us to understand the true beauty of the Bible message without using it to condemn others' conduct or to assume exalted positions over others who haven't studied its hidden truths. But half our Bible study class rebelled at this reasoned approach to God's word and apparently felt that they knew what God was trying to say better than anyone else; if one invited other interpretations of God's word other than theirs, then they weren't interested in pursuing Bible study.

"I have tried to bring you insights into another realm of consciousness where we can learn to replace competition with cooperation, where we can replace greed with selflessness, where love will motivate all of our actions rather than business as usual. I have tried to make every decision in our church based not upon whether it will bring in more money for the budget but whether it awakens us to the Holy Spirit's presence. I wish you well as you receive another shepherd, but I do not wish you comfort. I wish you wisdom, but I do not wish you self-satisfaction. I pray that you receive inspiration and not that you fall back on conformity to old habits. Keep in mind that each of you is embarked on a great journey and that the journey does not end with the funeral eulogy. Each of us is at a way-station. The question is, do we press on toward the goal of a unity with the Creator or do we wander in the moors of self-sufficiency and self-satisfaction? I hope in my brief stay with you that I have instilled in you the gift of an inquiring mind and a restless curiosity. I hope and pray that as a result of my tenure here you will, each of you, be forever changed and forever vigilant to God's presence among you and to God's plan for your life."

Kit slowly closed the Bible on the pulpit, bowed his head in a moment of silent prayer, and in dramatic silence proceeded down the steps from the altar and up the center aisle to the rear of the sanctuary. He noticed tears on many faces, some averted their gaze from him, others arose as if to greet him as he passed by, but no word was spoken. As he passed the pew in which Jean was sitting, she joined him and hand in hand, with heads held high, they together walked those final steps to the foyer of the church where he had so often geeted his parishioners after services. This time was different, however, as he stopped to greet no one.

A silent procession had fallen into step behind him and Jean as they made their way down the front steps of the church and into the fading light of day. No one counted the church members who joined the procession as compared to those who sat stunned in their pews or who slid silently out the side door of the sanctuary, but a turning point had been reached in the life of the church. A miracle occurred that day in the First United Methodist Church of Galilee, Missouri, and many said they were sure they saw Jesus himself walking with Kit and Jean as they left the quiet streets of the city and ascended the hill silouetted against the setting sun. It was a day to be remembered.